American

TANGO

A NOVEL

By

JENNIFER VANDEVER

Published in the United States by Melograno Press, Los Angeles

ISBN: 978-0-9966795-2-7

Cover design by Alison Halstead-Reid
Additional design by Amie Ziner
Book layout by ebooklaunch.com

www.jennifervandever.com

First Paperback Edition

Praise for Jennifer Vandever's **The Brontë Project**

A zippy romp in which Vandever skillfully parodies academia and Hollywood... Witty and artful.
Chelsea Cain, New York Times Book Review

A brilliant first novel of love: so original, so enchanting, so poignantly true that it defies you to put it down.
Karen Quinn (author of THE IVY CHRONICLES)

A first novel that is fresh, playful, intelligent, and consistently entertaining. *The Boston Globe*

A sweet read even a *Wuthering Heights* fan can love. *Entertainment Weekly*

A rollicking romp through the fun-house hallways of academe and the narcissism of celebrity. *Kirkus Reviews*

Wickedly clever...Vandever's irreverent debut novel dips into Victorian letters for inspiration, dredging up romantic angst to frame and foil a love story set in the age of new media. *Publishers Weekly*

Sometimes it seems, you can have it all... The Brontë Project is a silver-screen ready romp... the novel's dissection of the gulf between the myth of romance and the reality of love (using heroines as disparate as Princess Diana and Bronte herself as case studies) is the real — and really affecting — deal. *Elle*

It's never anything short of lovely to find a new writer like Vandever: funny, witty, smart, thoughtful... You'll want to see more from Vandever and soon. *Buffalo News*

Wickedly funny. *Christian Science Monitor*

In loving memory,

William Mathewson Vandever
(1929-2015)

part one

The forms of tango are like stages of a marriage. The American Tango is like the beginning of a love affair, when you're both very romantic and on your best behavior. The Argentine Tango is when you're in the heat of things and all kinds of emotions are flying: passion, anger, humor. The International Tango is like the end of the marriage, when you're staying together for the sake of the children.

— Barbara Garvey, *Smithsonian*

one

THAT'S JUST HOW IT IS. You get halfway through your life and realize you've done it all wrong. You've picked the wrong jobs and followed the wrong dreams. Every decision from your cradle to the counter of an upscale children's boutique in Portland, Oregon gratingly named *little fig* where you now stand tethered at the age of thirty-seven for thirteen-dollars-an-hour-plus-commission has been all wrong. Rosalind had just formed this thought as a new song came over the speakers.

That summer feeling, that summer feeling…

The store was empty; a customer might at least take her mind off things. *That summer feeling is gonna haunt you one day in your life*, Jonathan Richman's melancholy voice warned prophetically from the iPod behind the counter. Ingrid, the store's owner, had carefully selected a playlist that she thought would appeal to the store's natural demographic of parents in their thirties and forties who were affluent enough to buy a $25 onesie with an image of The Ramones or Che Guevara stenciled onto it.

That summer feeling, that summer feeling —

She got up from her stool and was about to select a new song when three teenagers stopped outside the doorway, debating whether or not to enter. They joked, they teased. They had nowhere to be. One girl seemed to be convincing the others. No one seemed too eager to go or stay. They might just stand there and argue the point all day. One girl erupted in hilarity. One rolled her eyes. The Friday afternoon of a teenager — had anything more wonderful ever existed? The first girl, the one who had been doing the convincing finally gave up on her friends and came in the store on her own.

"Hi. Can I help you find anything?" Rosalind asked, doubting the girl had any intention of buying something. The rain had finally let up and gathered in tidy pools around the entrance where the girl's friends stood, watching her through the window as if she'd entered on a dare.

"Maybe in a minute," the girl responded, as if sensing Rosalind's skepticism.

"Let me know if you need help."

The girl, wearing Doc Martens and an army green vintage overcoat, didn't look the type to be buying any of their merchandise. Even though *little fig* was located in the heart of the Pearl District, a trendy neighborhood once industrial and now known for its upscale boutiques and restaurants, customers were often shocked at the prices. They would pick up a hand-made sweater, simply charmed, and then turn over the price and return it to the rack with an insulted look. The nerve, their faces said, the nerve of that sweater being so overpriced! Doesn't that sweater know how quickly children grow? It got so Rosalind could tell just by looking if a person would be outraged by a $125 cashmere hoodie for an infant.

The girl held one up. She seemed undisturbed by the price, examining other colors. She noticed Rosalind watching her. Rosalind smiled and looked down. This was one of the problems with a small store: what to do with your eyes. Sometimes there was some bookkeeping to be done — she helped Ingrid out with this for extra money — or another customer to help. To sit and read seemed unprofessional. Usually she would doodle, sketching out ideas she had for a painting she might get around to doing someday. She did less and less of that anymore.

"Does this come in sizes for newborns?"

Rosalind looked up to see her holding one of the Che Guevara onesies. The girl's friends had now also joined her at the table of stenciled baby clothes.

"Everything we have is out there right now," Rosalind told her. "We're supposed to be getting a new shipment in next week if you want me to hold one for you."

The girl shook her head. They were all spending more time in the store than Rosalind would've guessed — maybe one of them was pregnant?

"Are you looking for something special? Maybe I can help," Rosalind offered, approaching the girls.

One folded up the Che onesie with contempt, telling her friend, "You don't want that anyway. Che Guevara is like Hitler only Cuban."

"Yeah," the other friend agreed, "Hitler only with mojitos."

The girl had dutifully moved on to a stack of Sex Pistols onesies — one of their biggest sellers.

"My brother-in-law would like this one — he thinks he's all punk rock even though he's just this douche working at Nike," she told Rosalind.

"Yeah, it's big with douches at Nike," Rosalind agreed with a laugh. The girl in the green coat seemed to relax to her.

"D'you have this for a newborn?"

"I'm sure we do," Rosalind assured her, rooting through stacks and finding one. "Your sister's expecting?"

The girl nodded as though this had not been welcome news to her.

"Yeah, the shower's this weekend. I've been doing so much planning, I totally forgot a gift. I think I'm just gonna go with the hoodie," she said, nodding at the table of pastel sweaters.

"Good choice," Rosalind assured her, calculating the commission in her head. She never steered shoppers towards the more expensive items but she always felt a small thrill when one easily fell onto the counter.

"Would you like this gift wrapped?"

The girl nodded.

"How will you be paying?" Rosalind asked after she had wrapped the peach hoodie in matching peach and coral tissue and tied it up with their special "*little fig*" embossed ribbon.

The girl slapped down a credit card with an ease that gave Rosalind a familiar twinge of jealously. There seemed to be an endless supply of such people buying overpriced onesies.

"How much are those?" the girl asked, nodding to a row of paintings on the wall. They were Rosalind's hummingbird series, a project she'd begun ironically, a contribution to a show challenging assumptions about feminine beauty. Rosalind had painted a set of hummingbirds hovering over intricate flowers on squares of pastel canvas, detailed with Victorian prettiness. They were the only things she painted that had ever sold. Now she had a going sideline, painting half a dozen a month for *little fig*, paintings she once felt superior to were now the only painting she did.

"They're $95.00," Rosalind told her.

"A *piece*?" she asked, seemingly affronted.

Rosalind nodded. "They're hand-painted by a local artist," she said, the word "artist" catching slightly in her throat.

"Who?"

"Rosalind Plumley."

The girl scrunched her nose. "Who is that?"

This gave Rosalind an unwelcome existential pang and so she launched into the spiel her husband Cal, the skilled marketer, had devised for her:

"Hummingbirds were believed by Native Americans to be magical emissaries from the afterlife. Some people like to keep these in the nursery as representative of someone who's passed — like a grandparent. As sort of a benevolent spirit."

The girl shook her head haughtily, "It's a little too soporific."

"Soporific?" one of her friends teased. "Where'd you get that? Let's get out of here, Thesaurus."

"What? It's real word," green coat said. "My niece is gonna grow up with real art, not cute stuff like that."

Rosalind rang up the clothes, trying to appear unmoved. But her ears were ringing with judgment. Why did she care what this girl thought? Rosalind used to imagine adjectives like "daring," "thought provoking," "challenging" dangling effortlessly from her work. She had the briefest impulse to defend herself, to tell the girl about the ironic interrogation of femininity going on in her painting. But she didn't. She was mediocre and green coat could smell it.

"Che Guevara was actually Argentinean," Rosalind said, swiping the girl's credit card.

"What?" she asked, disinterested.

"Your friend said he was Cuban."

The girl nodded her head indifferently and signed for her purchase. "What's this music?" she asked.

"Jonathan Richman," Rosalind told her. Remember when telling people who Jonathan Richman was made you feel cooler than whoever you were talking to? Rosalind thought. Well, now it makes you feel older.

"Oh," the girl said and headed out into the late afternoon with her friends.

Rosalind sighed and checked the time. Two more hours before the end of her shift. She stared up at her soporific painting, studying the little card underneath with her name and the price: Rosalind Plumley, $95. That about summed things up. Rosalind Plumley. That name! It made her think of crocheted doilies and gravy boats and grande dames of the English theatre. For this she received little sympathy from her older sister who'd been stuck with the far more cumbersome Hermione and barely a flicker of recognition from her younger sister Paulina, now Polly. Great heroines of Shakespeare. It was an idiot plan, they all decided, formulated by their mother, an English professor, whose stated mission had been to encourage her daughters in the direction of greatness. Her daughters would have lives of courage and wit and wonder. The unfolding beauty of the world would be their sole preoccupation. They would venture bravely towards bright futures. They would not stare disconsolately at the formation of raindrops on store windows longing for six o'clock.

The store was empty so she pulled out her phone and called Cal.

"Hey," he answered.

"How's the writing going?" she asked. She could hear the TV on in the background.

"Oh, you know. Slow. Glen's over."

Glen was always over.

"Don't forget we've got my parents' party tonight," she reminded him.

"Oh, right."

He'd forgotten.

"I sold one of those crazy expensive hoodies today," she said brightly.

"Awesome."

When Rosalind met Cal she thought he was too good to be true. She tried to remember that as she walked in their front door to find him splayed on their sofa, stoned. Again. He had recently arranged with his job as a copywriter for an outdoor apparel company, DimeEdge, to take one day off a week to work on his screenplay. But for two months this amounted to little more than watching movies and getting stoned with his friend Glen. Rosalind passed through the kitchen, noting the remains of his breakfast; yellow eggy residue hardening on plates resting in the sink, the good plates they'd gotten when they were married. So many sins in one sink!

Cal was depressed and tumbling, as was the standard practice, from one anti-depressant to the next; one made him jumpy, another gave him bad dreams. The latest seemed to curb his anxiety but gutted his libido. Even though the doctor had told them to start trying to get pregnant again, they hardly ever had sex anymore. The days off he had negotiated with his boss were supposed to improve his mood. A day of writing might be enough to clear his head, Rosalind had hoped, to get him back to his life's passion or whatever it was that he was missing. But he never wrote. He was still outlining or "conceiving," he told her. Actually, he was getting stoned with Glen.

Since his depression began he'd put on twenty pounds, a byproduct he claimed of the anti-depressants. The first ten pounds hadn't really bothered her. Cal had always been absurdly athletic, the type to see three hours of rock-climbing as a prelude to something really challenging. You can gain ten pounds without really noticing, she reasoned. But you gain ten more because something's happened.

"Remember the good times — you'll need them during the bad," a family friend had boozily warned her at their wedding. She'd thought the comment inappropriate at the time. Now she rolled the same handful of memories over and over in her head:

1) They met at a barbeque. He was new to Portland. He'd been invited by a college friend and Rosalind noticed him at once. Watching him, she joked with her sister Hermione that he was "J. Crew handsome" and standing next to the grill, he looked like he was in a catalog. Rosalind spent a good chunk of the party speculating with her sister about the kind of woman he'd be with.

"Her name's Sophie and she hikes and bakes bread. In fact, she bakes a lot but she never gains weight," Rosalind surmised.

"She's fluent in French," Hermione added.

"Yes. No. Russian. Italian? She studied abroad in Florence in college and met the only other man she's ever loved. It didn't work out but they're still friends. She's from a big family that summers in Montauk or something," Rosalind mused. "She has a nickname, something really annoying and East Coast like 'Plum' after a great-great-grandfather who built the railroads. Everyone loves her because she's genuinely nice but it's annoying because she's so perfect and it seems like her life is just charmed."

"Until she's in her forties and she has a son die of bone cancer," Hermione added. Hermione always took this game to a dark place. "Then forever after she has this kind of luminous quality that makes her seem fragile and beautiful."

"Uh, yeah. 'Poor Plum,' everyone will say. He'll love her even more after that."

"You're putting a lot of energy into this guy's marriage," Hermione observed. "Maybe you should say hello."

Rosalind dismissed this. She was no competition for Plum. But he introduced himself later. He was a writer. He was working in marketing for a new company called DimeEdge. She'd had a few and feeling too free, jokingly briefed him on his future wife. She was being condescending to mask her attraction. He was surprisingly gracious.

"Her name's 'Plum.' It's an old family name."

"She sounds awesome. D'you have her number?" he'd asked, amused.

"Sorry."

"What's your name?"

"Rosalind."

"Rosalind what?"

"Plumley."

"So a nickname for you might be Plum?"

"Oh, I didn't mean me!" she'd protested but too late, she could feel a mortifying blush spread across her face. She'd cast herself, unwittingly, as his perfect mate.

But he was so lovely, so good natured and casual about the whole thing. He smiled. She hadn't revealed too much. She'd given him just enough confidence to say, "Then maybe I should get your number."

2) They'd seen each other for a few weeks when Cal revealed that his only sibling, Jordy had died in a hiking accident. Cal had been 18 and Jordy, 15. They were going on their first solo climb up Mt. Hood. Jordy twisted an ankle and couldn't walk. Cal went for help. A storm picked up and it took two days for them to find Jordy's body. Cal had never stopped blaming himself even though he knew he'd done the right thing, leaving for help. His mother died of ovarian cancer two years later but Cal knew the real cause. A person can die of grief, he said. He'd seen it. Every Christmas he sent a personal hand-written note to every person who'd participated in the search, over fifty people. He had been doing this for ten years when Rosalind met him.

"Cal, we've got the party in just an hour," she reminded, she hoped, gently.

"Glen has this sore we're trying to decide if he needs to go to the doctor for," Cal said, motioning to a supremely relaxed Glen, his large, hairy frame tucked into an armchair. Glen was like a summer cold — he never went away and it was never clear where he'd come from in the first place.

"Where is it?" Rosalind asked reluctantly. Glen shrugged. This was how it was with Glen: too much information followed by too little.

"Does it hurt?" Rosalind asked charitably. In Glen's stupor, pain seemed an unlikely prospect.

"No, think I'll just put an ace bandage on it when I get home." An ace bandage was Glen's answer to everything.

"D'you want me to give you a ride home?" Rosalind offered, hoping for a refusal.

"Naw," he said, rising unsteadily. Cal studied the ceiling attentively.

Glen nodded thoughtfully and launched on a brief expedition for his shoes. He had never revealed the location of his sore and now Rosalind worried it had seeped into their furniture, in this case a second-hand armchair covered — like everything else in their home it seemed — with a chenille throw. No spots, Rosalind noted with relief.

"Are you OK getting home on your bike?" she asked him, shoes found, as he lumbered towards the front door where the bright post-rain sunlight appeared to assault him. He had recently had his license revoked on a DUI and now used his nine-year-old niece's bicycle to get around.

"Yeah, you're a sweetheart. Have fun, you two."

Rosalind smiled as she watched him lurch forward onto the sidewalk — he looked like a circus act, a bear on a tiny bicycle. He waved behind him and Rosalind closed the front door, turning to really take in Cal.

"Cal? How stoned are you?"

"Just kinda. Don't worry. I'm fiiiine." He fixed her with a smile. "I bought you sad flowers," he said, nodding to a handful of limp-headed daisies straining against gravity in a wide-mouthed vase on the coffee table.

"Oh! Sad flowers," Rosalind said, finally noticing them. "You know, we have nicer looking daisies growing in the backyard."

"Yeah," he acknowledged guiltily. "I know."

The sad flowers were a regular indulgence purchased from a store Cal and Rosalind called the "saddest flower store in the world." It was just down the block from their house in what was now a fashionable stretch of southeast Portland. The saddest flower store in the world was the last lone holdout from a vanishing era now replaced by wine bars and stores selling artisanal farm-to-cone ice cream. If the sad looking flowers didn't chase away the customers, its owner did; Mr. Hoffman was a perpetually red-faced man given to loud, profanity-laced arguments with his daughter over the phone. They felt bad about the gentrification that was steadily driving out the old Chinese restaurants and vacuum repair shops and sad flower stores, and regularly stopped in, listening patiently to Mr. Hoffman's strong opinions on his daughter's boyfriend (no good, probably a drug dealer) and the unfortunate changes in the neighborhood, even though Cal in his $200 (before the 30% employee discount, but still...) DimeEdge fleece-lined windbreaker was symptom A of said gentrification.

"There's hardly any flowers — he mostly gave you greens," Rosalind said. She admired Cal's commitment to the store but even she had her limits.

"I know. At least the greens are fresh."

"Maybe in a vase with a narrower mouth?" she said, studying the browning stalks struggling to support the weight of their wilting heads.

"That's the wrong vase?" he asked, sounding oddly wounded by this information.

"No, no," she added hastily, aware that she was diminishing the kindness of the flowers with the wrongness of the vase. "It's perfect. They're lovely. Thank you."

"Come here, you," he ordered, playfully pulling her towards him. She gave him a peck on the lips, the only kind of physical affection they shared lately.

"You look nice," he told her.

She looked at him, readying herself to return the compliment and noticed how pale and washed out he looked. He had always been so athletic and ruddy-faced it was strange to see him now fading into the sofa. But he had saved her, she reminded herself. Saved her from a succession of musician boyfriends — all, strangely, bassists — so distant and unreliable that the electric guitar had become for her the sound of male inattention. A man who saved you from bassists should be allowed to be pale for a few months, she reasoned.

"You look good too," she told him.

"Ha," he snickered sarcastically. "I'm fat."

"You are not. 'Sides you'll get back in shape soon. So will I."

He nodded, unconvinced.

"Get any writing done?"

"S'more outlining," he said vaguely.

Rosalind smiled, noting the skunky scent in the air.

"I sold one of those cashmere hoodies today," she said.

"You said. Congrats!"

She had already told him, she remembered now. How sad that this was the highlight of her day. She didn't mention the girl who called her paintings cute and soporific.

He gave a her a long kiss, the kind they used to have before the troubles. He looked her over. "I like this shirt. Did I buy you this shirt?"

"When have you ever bought me a shirt?" she asked. She had dug it out from the back of her closet, a pink vintage blouse with a scalloped neck and a fitted waist. She still had a few items she wore from her twenties when she pored over second-hand stores to affect a 1930's look, cutting her dark curly hair chin length and wearing bias cut skirts that worked on her tall, long-waisted frame. But these days she settled for a khaki or denim skirt (she'd alternated them all week during the unseasonably hot ninety degree days that'd turned suddenly to rain) and a simple cotton shirt. Her days of making an effort on clothes were over.

"Maybe I'll start," he said, making this sound like a naughty threat. He kissed her again. She laughed gently.

"What's this? Are you...?" she asked, surprised.

"Kinda."

"You're never stoned *and* horny," she said, kissing him again.

"What time's the party?"

"We can be late," she said, still kissing him.

two

"JESUS, YOU SMELL like sex, Ros," Polly said as she hugged her sister hello. "I thought you two never did it now you're on those boner killer pills," she said to Cal as he followed Rosalind through the door.

"Hey, Polly. Good to see you too," Cal sighed, giving Rosalind an aggrieved look.

"Y'know — don't have to say everything that comes into your head, Polly." Rosalind said.

Polly shrugged her indifference. She was dressed up in chunky black boots and what looked like a prom dress from the 50's, a chiffon colored bodice giving way to plumes of mint green. She took after their mother and was short and bosomy, unlike Hermione and Rosalind who took after their tall, lanky father.

"Least I know why you're late," Polly said.

"How's it going?"

Polly looked heavenward and sighed as if recalling an ancient trauma.

"Same as every year. Mom's in the kitchen with her disciples and Dad's — I don't know — probably with Jerry somewhere getting high."

"Hermione?"

"Upstairs. Sleeping. Her plane got in late."

Rosalind looked out across the crowd of academics and artists in their sixties, her parents' usual. When she brought Cal to his first unniversary party she explained the crowd as the "type with old Volvos with John Kerry bumper stickers still on them." There were always a few former and current students of her mother's, usually stylish young women, clustered around her in the kitchen, sipping moderately priced Pinot Grigio and laughing about men or Fox News. The ritual of the "unniversary party" required an explanation in itself. Like most of the family jokes it started as an ironic nod to the stupidity of the term and then quickly became a tradition. Rosalind's parents had been effectively separated for over twenty years but chose to remain married and live under the same roof, her mother staying mostly on the upper story and her father occupying the basement and an outdoor artist's studio they'd built in the large backyard early in their marriage. The house was too large even when they were a family of five and it easily accommodated two people living separate lives who occasionally, amiably ran into one another in the kitchen.

The home had been purchased shortly after the birth of Hermione with an inheritance left to their mother. The neighborhood had transitioned into prime real estate, growing more fashionable with each decade until they were surrounded on all sides by affluent young families. The house occupied a prime chunk of the block, edging deep into its center with groves of trees, lazily maintained pots of flowers, and a swing-set and jungle gym abandoned by the Plumley girls thirty years earlier. Plastic furniture was scattered around indifferently, a careless but nevertheless pointed indictment of the tasteful Adirondack chairs and Japanese maples and sprays of well-tended flowers that filled the lots of neighboring lawns. Only Mrs. Matacek, a widow in a tidy one-story house down the block had lived on their street as long. But she was not loved like the Plumleys. She was unfriendly, didn't compost and was known to hose down her driveway during droughts. But the Plumleys attracted neighbors who would sit down on the couch and find themselves still there, hours later, inexplicably immobile, caught up in conversation. And they sat there tonight, Rosalind noted as she hung up her jacket on one of the hooks that lined the long entryway. There was always someone new around, her mother collected these people.

"I'm gonna walk around," Cal said and Rosalind knew this was code for "find someone with weed."

"Cal," she said.

"What?"

"You have to drive home, OK?" The argument was as traditional as the unniversary party itself: who, between Rosalind and Cal, deserved to overindulge. Rosalind would argue the party was the culmination of all that was crazy about her family but Cal would argue that he was being the patient spouse and therefore the responsibility of designated driver was hers. Rosalind liked to believe her indulgence of his sour moods and lack of sex for the past couple months brought a little extra credit to her account. But she realized, as she watched the back of his head disappear into the kitchen their brief return to sex restored the balance.

"Well, screw him," Polly said, thrusting a glass of wine in Rosalind's hand. Polly was good at this, pushing you towards decisions that were probably unwise. "Get drunk."

"Thanks," said Rosalind, sipping cautiously.

"Why not just stay the night? Everyone else does."

"That's why."

Polly scoffed. Almost thirty, she had still never lived on her own, always passing through the apartments and shared houses of boyfriends or schoolmates and then returning to her old bedroom in the Plumley house. She pretended to hate the arrangement even though it suited her. She couldn't finish college or hold a job or maintain a relationship for long. She could never find employment that didn't fatally compromise her morals or a boyfriend who didn't disappoint.

As Rosalind moved towards the kitchen she could already hear her mother's voice, animated over the din of happy, wine-soaked admirers.

"Well, that's just it, isn't it? Men and their erections! Nothing more sacred," her mother, Helen exclaimed. It sounded like one of her usual rants, though she was surprised to see it directed at Cal, who stood flush against the kitchen counter surrounded by women. Helen had a talent for this, extracting intimate details in a short period of time. She would pull them out, piece by piece, lining them up like car parts in a driveway, and then go to work deducing how the patriarchy had brought them about. During his brief visit to the kitchen she had apparently gotten into Rosalind's miscarriage and the money they were saving up because his company's health plan didn't cover fertility treatments but did, unjustly it seemed to her, Viagra.

"I can totally believe your plan would cover erections. I mean, of course!" Helen said, the outrage of it all making her cheeks red with emotion. Helen wasn't tall but she seemed always to stand above others. Her gray hair had long been worn in a neat pageboy that grazed her chin and she wore one of her usual loose neutral-toned rayon tunic and skirt combos dressed up for the occasion with low heels, large silver Mexican earrings and a lapis lazuli pendant around her neck.

"Why cover wombs when you could give money to men and their dicks?" Helen asked rhetorically as everyone nodded. "Nothing more sacred!"

"Maybe you both should try not eating wheat," one of Helen's old students, a pale woman in her thirties, told Cal.

"Dairy!" another woman advised. "I gave up dairy and sugar and two months later I was pregnant!"

Cal nodded. He would definitely look into it. Rosalind could see him eyeing the fire pit through the kitchen window longingly.

"There you are, sweetheart! We were just talking about your womb," Helen said affectionately, pulling Rosalind into a tight embrace. Like many offspring of the aggressively open, Rosalind was by nature deeply private. She resented her mother's indiscretion but smiled just the same. And screw Cal, she thought. She was going to get drunk.

"Hi, Mom."

"You're perfect the way you are. You don't want to go having babies. Babies ruin everything." Helen said this often and jokingly but it was never a joke Rosalind found all that funny. "And you, my Callum" she said, turning to Cal, ready to complete her diagnosis, "need to quit that job. Stay home. Write your screenplay. You could live here! Cal's working on a screenplay," she told her audience. "It's brilliant."

"Thanks, Helen - but you haven't read it," Cal protested, good-natured.

"It's about... what's his name?"

"Ilia Ivanov. Real guy," Cal explained to them. "He did all kinds of genetic experiments in the early 20th century. He created the zeedonk — half zebra, half donkey."

Rosalind had heard this story many times but it was nice to see Cal so animated.

"Stalin hires him to breed a half man-half ape race. But it didn't work. Turns out even though we share, like, 96% of our genes, the way our chromosomes are ordered just doesn't work."

The ladies nodded their heads politely.

"That's what you should be working on instead of worrying about babies," Helen told him.

"Thanks, Mom, but we'll figure it out," Rosalind said. She hated when her mother did this, played the supportive, groovy mom when she was actually just mortifying her daughter.

"Oh, well," her mother sighed, unable to understand why anyone would want to live anywhere else. "It's up to you. But you're always welcome. Where's Richard?" she asked anyone within hearing range. "I hope he's not getting stoned before our toasts. Did you try the eggplant caponata? I had everything catered this year by Patty's daughter, Amy. You know, the one that was on drugs? She cleaned up and she's in cooking school now. I'm trying to be supportive. I wonder where the hell is Richard?" she asked again, though she seemed only vaguely interested in the answer. Rosalind looked up from her glass and noticed Cal had disappeared as well.

Stepping outside, Rosalind pulled her sweater up against her bare neck. The June night was cool and the afternoon rain had left the yard damp. Smokers stood in intimate groups of twos and threes but Cal was not among them. Rosalind smiled and waved in passing, hoping not to be stopped or pulled into conversation. She made her way to the outer depths of the yard, past the light of the fire pit and the tiki torches set around the perimeter of garden chairs. She was tired of people already and the evening had only just begun. It took so much energy to appear normal. She saw the light on in her father's studio — party-goers often ended up there late in the evening, drinking whiskey and trying to extract meaning from the large brown and gray canvases he had specialized in painting for the last decade.

The urgency to find Cal left her. She paused in the dark space between the house and fire-lit patio and the glow of her father's studio, out of anyone's sight. She could stay right here forever if it were only allowed — poised between scenes during a night that required many, an actor enjoying a stolen moment in the wings. She inhaled the night deeply. The sweet dank smell of marijuana and cigarettes and the beginning of summer filled her with a sense: there was a life underneath this life, the real life. And she'd lost it.

"Rosalind!"

Voices echoed in this part of the yard bordered by the garage, the studio and the thick trunks of firs and maples and oaks — a feature the young Plumley girls once delighted in teasing one another with. As a child, Rosalind had consulted one of her mother's mythology books and developed a firm conviction that woodland spirits did indeed exist. She'd talk to them for hours out here among the trees. Maybe they were talking to her now, urging her to action.

"Rosalind!"

Rosalind looked around.

"Rosalind!" the voice said again.

"Trees?" she answered, uncertainly.

"Ros, stop being weird. C'mere!"

Rosalind turned to see Hermione framed in the doorway of the studio watching her deranged sister addressing the canopy of trees.

"I thought you were asleep," Rosalind said.

"I was. C'mere."

"Hi," she said, giving her sister a hug as she joined her in the studio. Their father had tidied up for the evening. The space was no larger than a small garage and except for parties, no one but he ever spent any time in it. He had works in progress propped unself-consciously along one wall. He prided himself on this lack of vanity; he could share any work at any time. Lately he had been painting enormous canvases that were really only limited by the dimensions of his workspace, in moody grays which merged with irides-cent layers of charcoal and black.

Hermione took a good look at one, cocking her head the way she did when she disapproved.

"It's like a Wellbutrin ad in here. Let's go outside," Hermione suggested. Rosalind followed her to a forgotten swing-set; the space underneath each swing, once deep ruts from the girls' feet, had long been reclaimed by tall grass and dandelions. Hermione took one and Rosalind sat next to her.

"Nice of you to come back," Rosalind said. "I know it means a lot to them."

"It's the fortieth. Couldn't miss that," she said.

"No," Rosalind said, laughing. "I guess not."

Both sisters fell silent, meaning they both had much to say. Instead, they smiled hesitantly, as if daring the other to start with her news. Rosalind took a deep breath and finished her wine.

"I'm going to go get more. Can I get you some?"

"No. I'm not drinking."

"Not drinking at an unniversary party? You're brave."

"Actually... I'm pregnant."

"Oh," Rosalind said, aware that she was frowning when she should be smiling.

"That's your response?" Hermione said, teasing.

"No, of course not," Rosalind said, standing and making her sister do the same so she could give her a hug. "Congratulations! That's so great. I mean, you're keeping it, right?"

"Duh."

"Well. You never know. That's great. You'll be a great mom," Rosalind said, aware of her tight smile and that she kept saying "great."

"I hope so. We didn't have the best model to work with."

"They're good parents. Mostly. Well, I mean, mom's, y'know —" said Rosalind.

"Overbearing? Narcissistic? They should've divorced twenty years ago and here we are celebrating... what? That they're too cowardly to move on with their lives?"

"Well," said Rosalind, raising her hand to indicate the voice of reason. "Dad needs the health insurance and there's the house —"

"This house! Why the huge house? Still?"

"How far along are you?" Rosalind asked, moving off a historically unsolvable impasse.

"I'm almost through my first trimester."

Rosalind felt a wave of sorrow; she remembered telling people that.

"You're not showing."

"Are you kidding? I'm huge," Hermione said, pointing to a barely perceptible bump under her shirt. Hermione had always been the pretty one; tall, willowy with dark blond curly hair that contrasted with the rest of the dark-haired Plumleys. She had moved to France on a scholarship to study theater with a director Hermione said was famous but no one had actually heard of. He was a follower of the Polish theatrical pioneer, Jerzy Grotowski and of penetrating, socially conscious theater meant to confront and challenge its audience. Rosalind had traveled to Paris once to see one of her plays which featured a barely dressed Hermione hurling racial epithets at the audience and dry humping a black doll. Rosalind, like most of the Plumleys, fiercely admired Hermione's daring while being secretly happy her productions took place overseas, providing a ready excuse for missing them.

"Are you and Cal still trying?"

"Yeah. Sort of. Not so much."

Hermione gave her a look of concern but Rosalind waved it away.

"Well, at least you weren't that far along," Hermione said. "You can try again."

"I was about as far along as you," Rosalind reminded her tersely.

"Jesus. You're right. I'm sorry," Hermione could be a jerk but she always fixed it right away. It was one of the things Rosalind had loved about her. Back when they were close. "I really am sorry 'bout what happened. I have a friend in Paris who miscarried three times who just had a baby girl. Don't give up! It'll happen."

It'll happen. That's what everyone said. Rosalind smiled. "Are you moving back to the states?" she asked.

"Why?"

"Well, I mean, can you afford a kid? Doing experimental theater?"

"I make a lot of money actually."

Hermione looked down at the ground and then leveled her gaze at her sister with a look that indicated far bigger revelations were on the way. Rosalind steeled herself for the real story, how her sister *actually* supported herself all these years — sordid, ugly tales of cocaine transported in bowels or blowjobs given to Parisian businessmen in the backs of minivans.

"I'm a pharmaceutical rep."

"Jesus! *Really?*"

"Yeah," Hermione said, nodding soberly.

"Do mom and dad know?"

"Are you kidding? They'd shit themselves."

"How long?"

"A little over a year ago. I started out in human resources —"

"Human resources? Hermione! This is *unbelievable*."

"I know, I know."

"What about the father? Do I know him?" then recalling Hermione's wilder days thought to ask, "Do *you* know him?"

"You met him a few years ago. Laurent?"

Rosalind shook her head. She had no memory of him.

"We were just friends at the time. He's really sweet. He's not like the guys I used to date. I mean, like, he designs software. But you know, he's great. It's like one day you wake up and realize you wanna date a grown up. When Laurent says he's gonna be somewhere, he is. Early. With groceries!"

"Are you getting married?"

"We already did."

"Hermione!"

That stung. Only two years apart, they'd always shared everything.

"I'm sorry, Ros. I tried to tell you but you and Cal were dealing with so much and I didn't want to tell Helen just yet and I didn't want to put you in the middle of anything…"

Rosalind gave her a wounded look.

"It was shitty, I know," Hermione admitted. "I should've told you. I would have but you seemed like you had enough on your plate and I figured I'd tell everyone in person during my visit. Or at least you," she said, reaching out and squeezing Rosalind's hand.

"You have to tell them," Rosalind summed up with a sigh, looking out across the backyard. She could hear her mom's friend Karin gathering people to come inside. It was probably time for the toasts.

"I will. I mean, I'm telling them about the pregnancy — though I don't even want to do that. Look at how much shit mom gave you about being pregnant. I don't know if I can go into the husband and the job and the house in the suburbs."

"You have a *house*? In the *suburbs*?"

Hermione nodded. Rosalind's resentment finally found its hold.

"Hermione, I have been the white sheep of this family for years with the marriage and the mortgage and you're telling me you're even more conventional than me? D'you know how much shit I get?"

"I know."

"I thought you were doing street theater and eating out of garbage cans. We all did! Don't mom and dad still send you money?"

Hermione nodded guiltily.

"I donate it to Doctors Without Borders. I figure they'd want it that way."

"Wow," Rosalind finally managed, stunned. "What about that horrible little apartment? Isn't your mail still going there?"

"I have a girlfriend subletting it. She gives me my mail."

"Wow."

"I know. But Ros, you can't say anything."

"What about your acting?"

Hermione laughed a little bitterly and then stared off into the night.

"I realized theater was just this elaborate ruse for screwed up middle-aged guys to get laid. I mean, Anton," — this was the famous/not famous director — "and I were lovers for years and I was just so, so stupid. And it was just so screwed up. We'd 'tour' Europe — his word for it — and every city we'd go to there would be some breakfast with some random kid and some confused looking lady and he'd be like 'this is Remi, my son, this is Remi's mama.' Everywhere we went! Like he had a kid in every European capital. And would you believe, *he* left *me*!? That's how screwed up I was. I wanted to have a kid. Seriously, I wanted to join that sad, screwed up club. So we broke up. I was practically suicidal at the time — like I couldn't imagine life without this jerk, right? Crazy! And Laurent was there. He was such a good friend. He had a friend at a pharmaceutical company who gave me a job. I started washing my face again and eating. And then one night, I didn't even expect it, we made love. Just like that. We moved in together two weeks later." Hermione shrugged again. "I hated acting if you want to know the truth," she said. "That was mom and dad's fantasy. Always was." Hermione turned to her sister, realizing she'd done all the talking. "How are you?"

Rosalind shook her head casually. "I'm fine." She'd wanted to tell her more about the miscarriage and Cal and his sadness and the lack of sex except tonight which wasn't, on balance, all that great. She'd wanted, originally, to spend the evening drinking too much wine with her sister, catching up and telling everything. Or most everything. But now she regarded her sister with curious distance. She'd been so actively excluded from everything important to her she felt suddenly, intensely alone. Maybe someday, later, they would talk and laugh, remembering the time Hermione hid who she was. But not tonight.

Karin traipsed across the dark lawn. She had been Helen's best friend for decades, a speech therapist always, it seemed, in the middle of some new divorce. She swept her thick hair out of her eyes and stretched her arms out triumphantly.

"There you are. They're ready to make their toasts!"

Rosalind and Hermione joined the rest of the party in the dining room as people straggled in from far corners of the house and front porch and backyard. Helen was engaged in one of her favorite tirades about intelligent design.

"What I don't get," she said, directing her attention to Lance, an environmental lawyer who lived two doors down, but clearly addressing her crowd, "is if they're going to point to all the wonders of the world as evidence of a creator, how do they account for all the design flaws? I mean just look at the human body. The back? Terrible design. Knees? Penises?"

This elicited a roar of protest to which Helen smiled and slyly elaborated, "I mean, the proximity of the prostate causes all kinds of problems, later in life. Just ask Richard."

Richard Plumley sat silently at the table in his usual black jeans, black t-shirt under an unbuttoned denim shirt. He was tall, almost gaunt, with thinning gray hair. He nodded. Indeed, the prostate was unluckily located; he himself had struggled with prostate cancer over the years and Helen's excellent insurance from the university had been one of the many reasons cited for the Plumleys — though Helen had never given up her maiden name of Rourke — to stay married.

"Well, I'd say knees are definitely the work of the devil," Lance agreed, having spent the better part of the year dealing with a blown ACL.

"There's at least one good thing about where the prostate is," said her friend, Victor with an eyebrow raised suggestively. Victor was a professor of Gender and Media Studies.

"Oh, my God!" Helen said. "You mean anal?"

"Oh, yes."

"I had no idea! How can I be this old and not know about prostates and anal?"

"Happy fortieth, sweetheart," he said, raising a glass.

Rosalind and Hermione exchanged a glance. It was a typical Plumley party: God, penises, anal sex — all that was left was for someone to announce tragically that they'd run out of wine (no worries, there was always more in the basement!). Richard rose from his chair and observed his audience with shy apprehension. He always seemed a little surprised to find life going on outside his studio and now here it was, waiting for a toast.

"Borges says —" he began.

"Oh God, *Borges*?" Rosalind whispered to Hermione.

"That 'to fall in love is to create a religion with a fallible God.' The beauty of my forty plus years with this woman," he continued, slipping a hand uncertainly on the edge of Helen's shoulder, "is that we know we're fallible. And that's close enough to love."

The crowd clapped absently. The unniversary toasts were always a strange operation. How did you appropriately celebrate the ironic recognition of your failed marriage? It was all fun and vodka till the toasts rolled around and then there was often the grim realization that maybe, just maybe, this was all a terrible idea. Helen had one of her glazed smiles meaning she'd had too much wine to safely judge whether she'd just been insulted. She didn't want their fortieth to go down in what Rosalind liked to call a "full George and Martha."

"Love," she began provocatively, allowing the word to hang uncomfortably in the air, "is a strange thing that changes over time." Some people nodded anxiously: yes, yes, it really is. "Here's to forty years," she said, raising a glass, "of reading between the lines and trying to figure out what the hell Richard just said."

Everybody laughed. The evening was saved and the prosecco flowed. Richard and Helen hugged — they had mastered the art of being both familiar and distant at the same time. Watching them Rosalind felt a kind of sick premonition, a vision of what awaited her and Cal. These sad pretensions — why did they bother with them? It was a mystery to her even after all these years why they stayed together under one roof. She knew the excuses: it was never the right time to sell such a prize of a house, it suited them, Richard's freelance lifestyle and enlarged prostate required the health insurance of a tenured professor — but they never really made sense to her. Why not just buy condominiums and have the children celebrate two Christmases like all the other parents? Rosalind sensed pride at work and a misplaced fascination with being strange, being wonderfully odd, being *interesting*. She remembered asking Karin about it once, maybe hinting at a harsh judgment. Karin had just sighed and said, "You'd be surprised the number of arrangements between couples."

Rosalind surveyed the room. People hugged her parents, made jokes. Couples sat next to each other, neat dyads recounting trips to Spain and mysterious stomach pains and things remembered from the news. Her parents swayed to Louis Armstrong, a believable imitation of a couple happily wed for forty years. Other couples joined in the dancing. They were all a mystery, these couples and their complicated arrangements, understood by no one, negotiating midnight desires with their daytime selves. It's too late, Rosalind wanted to tell them, too late to pick up and make all new mistakes and blame it on youth and inexperience. That time was past and now every mistake counted, every misstep required a lawyer and an accountant, a new form at tax time. It was too late to think no one would hold it against you if you just ran away, ran and kept running. There would be change of address forms to fill out and the concerned looks of therapists staring down at the notes cataloging your foolishness.

"Is Cal still seeing a therapist?" she heard and turned to see Karin at her side.

Rosalind nodded. Helen had likely told her.

"Marriage is tough, you know? You think you're responsible for everything but you're not. Sometimes it's over, sometimes it's not." Karin gave a thrice-divorced worldly shrug.

"You think my marriage is over?" Rosalind asked, alarmed.

"No, I'm just saying you're on a path and sometimes the path goes down further and sometimes it stops."

Rosalind nodded silently. It was getting to be that part of the evening where people stared down at their drinks and doled out gloomy, possibly useless advice.

"People need to be known more than they need to be loved," Karin continued. "Like Mark" — her ex — "could not have been more obvious that he was cheating. Left out hotel receipts and his date-book even! Why would someone do that? He knows he'll lose love. But a person needs to be known. It's bigger than love. Maybe Cal needs to be known."

Rosalind nodded.

"You're both at that age," Karin said, looking at her, assessing, "where you're overwhelmed by all the things you'll never do."

"We are?" Rosalind asked.

"Think about the next thing. For both of you. If you want to be happy."

Rosalind let the words sink in, wine fogging her senses. Should she be irritated by the unsolicited advice? Or rush home and follow it to the letter?

"Rosalind!"

Rosalind's father was calling her from inside the house.

"Excuse me," Rosalind said, following her father's voice into the dining room where the family was gathered for a group photo.

"Approximate happiness!" he commanded, a family joke he always maintained, though the Plumley girls would roll their eyes.

Afterwards, he pulled Rosalind aside to thank her for her unniversary present, one of her hummingbird paintings.

"It's beautiful, Ros. Really beautiful."

"Thanks."

She couldn't think of anything else to give them but wished she hadn't now. Beautiful. It felt like an indictment, a reminder of her shallowness, her fatal eagerness to please. Beautiful. He meant it too. He was being supportive and lovely as usual. He'd always supported her work, refused to be competitive or nasty. She'd been a bit of a prodigy. Won contests and scholarships. She was supposed to be something. He never seemed to mind that she might eclipse his respectable but solidly unspectacular career. Now that she'd blown her earlier promise he was even more solicitous. She knew he didn't mean to be patronizing, but really? A pretty picture of a hummingbird? He had to be sad. He had to return to his studio late at night, pour himself a whiskey, sigh to himself and think, *I thought she was going to do something.* Her father, bless him, was too nice to say it.

"Well. Happy unniversary," she told him, trying to smile.

"Are you alright?" he asked.

"Yeah. Too much wine. I should find Cal," she said.

three

"*CAL.* YOU TOLD me it was OK to drink."

"It is. It was."

"You're stoned," Rosalind said, joining him in the car.

"I'm fine."

"I can't believe you went off and got stoned again."

"I'm not stoned."

"You know what Jerry's stuff does to you."

Cal sighed deeply. There was a brief silence and then the sound of Cal putting the key in the ignition.

"I can drive," Rosalind volunteered.

"Jesus, Plum. You're in no state to drive."

"Fine. We'll just call a cab," she said, reaching for the door's handle.

"Plum, could you go for maybe five seconds without pointing out what a failure I am? Could you possibly ever do that? Please? Jesus…"

The two fell silent again. Cal's outbursts, while not uncommon, were usually not directed at Rosalind. She felt a sick surge of anger. The injustice of it all. She had been so patient, so understanding and this was her thanks? She wiped away a hot tear; she didn't want to sit in front of the Plumley house crying, especially at an unniversary party. She tried to talk herself out of being upset as Cal started the car and nosed out into the street. He was a good driver. There wasn't any reason to worry. She worried too much, that was her problem. She and Cal would be fine. They didn't need a change like Karin said. Cal was just having a bad patch and she was making it worse with her incessant worrying and then she heard it. An awful thud.

Cal jolted the car to a stop.

"Shit. Oh, shit," he said softly, breathing deeply as he opened his car door. "Oh shit, oh shit, oh shit, oh shit."

Rosalind opened her door as well. The sound seemed like it had come from her side. It was so loud and awful. Rosalind kept hearing the sound replay in her head as she rounded the car door and looked down under the right wheel.

"Oh, Cal!"

"What is it?"

"A dog. You hit a dog."

"Oh, shit."

Cal knelt down next to the animal, a dark brown Labrador. Rosalind looked at him as he calmly assessed the dog. He pulled a first aid kit from the trunk, delicately cataloguing the dog's possible damage.

"He's stunned. Could be in shock. Could be bleeding internally."

Cal wrapped the dog's snout with a gauze bandage, in case he came to, he explained, dogs often bite in situations of stress. He excelled in moments of crisis like this; his years in wilderness emergency left him well equipped for disaster. She felt an electric surge of attraction for him she hadn't felt in months.

"Hey, Plum?"

"Yeah?"

"We're gonna have to move him," he said.

While she sat close by, stroking the dog, Cal found a picnic blanket in the backseat that he edged under the dog, motioning for her to grab the other side.

"Careful, gentle, shhhh," he told her and the dog as they carefully lifted the dog into their backseat.

"I think there's a 24-hour place on Sandy," Cal said, remembering.

There was in fact a 24-hour place on Sandy, outfitted with a glaring white waiting room in which Cal and Rosalind sat forlornly staring at advertisements for flea remedies. It was three a.m. and they were the only ones there. The veterinarian, a dour Asian man, simply nodded when they carried the dog in as though he'd been expecting them all along. When he finally emerged from the examination room he still had the same unhappy look. Rosalind wasn't sure what to read into this.

"You should really get him a chip. He doesn't have one," he told them, irritated with the whole lot of pet owners.

"He's not our dog," Rosalind reminded him for the third time.

"Oh," said the vet, nodding.

"How is he?" Cal asked.

The vet shrugged.

"He'll be OK. Some lacerations I cleaned up. Stunned mostly. Got a lot of degeneration in his knees — but guess that's not your problem."

"Is that from the accident?" Rosalind asked.

He shook his head. "Happens over time. 'Specially in your larger breeds like labs. He's probably 'bout six or seven so, yeah, that'll happen. Here's a list of local shelters you wanna take him to one."

"No," Cal assured him. "We'll take care of him till we find the owner."

The vet handed them a bill so exorbitant Rosalind gasped.

"I ran tests. Did blood work," the vet told her defensively.

"What kind of tests?" Rosalind asked, as though she were in any position to negotiate.

"You take credit cards?" Cal asked.

"Yeah," the vet nodded wearily and gestured to a fake wood counter where he rang up their bill.

"I think that vet was a little sketchy, don't you?" Rosalind asked as they drove home.

Cal exhaled his exasperation with the whole damned night.

"I guess a vet at three a.m.'s kinda like a plumber on Christmas," he said. "You take what you can get."

She nodded and turned around to check their new, very expensive guest in the backseat. He seemed to notice her gaze and raise his head from the seat where he'd been resting, fixing her with what seemed to be a complacent, almost menacing smile.

"He look like anyone to you?" Cal asked over breakfast the next morning. The dog had adopted a nearly spiritual attachment to Cal and rested peacefully at his feet.

"Karl Malden?" Rosalind asked.

Cal gave her a look.

"All dogs look like Karl Malden," she explained. "Don't you think?"

"I'm serious."

"I am too. I didn't tell you, Hermione's pregnant!"

He didn't look up from the dog.

"Hmn?"

"She's married. Lives in the suburbs. She's in *human resources*!"

"He doesn't look just like anyone to you?" he asked again.

"Hermione's a total bourgeois."

Cal nodded.

"I was talking to this woman at the party last night," Rosalind said, studying him, "friend of one of their neighbors or something. She told me — she must've been drunk — she told me she and her husband routinely had sex for twelve hours."

"Jesus," he sighed, cradling the dog's face in his hands. "Who's got that kind of time?"

"Well, she explained it's this thing where every act has intention. That's what *tantra* is, she said, expanding everything to its fullest expression. So you could, like, load the dishwasher and it could have sensual intent."

Cal looked up from the dog.

"Are you saying you want to have sex again? Or you want me to load the dishwasher?"

"*Again?* You say it like we're done for the year."

"The washer's loaded. I'll unload it when it's through, OK?"

She stared at him forlornly.

"What?" he asked, his voice tinged with exasperation. He rose and put on a jacket, opening the back door that led to the driveway.

"Where are you going?" she asked.

"Gonna see about getting a leash for this guy. Maybe go for a walk later," he said and walked out the door.

While Cal was out shopping, Rosalind turned to the pile of newspapers collecting on the dining room table and started leafing through the *New York Times* travel section left over from the previous Sunday. Thumbing through she noticed something that stopped her: a photo of a man and woman dancing the tango.

It was from a piece on Buenos Aires and all the young artistic people who had flocked there to live the life she should have been living if she had any sense or luck or whatever it took to be happy. In the photo the man's gaze was lowered, almost reverential. His right arm wrapped around the woman's bare upper back, gently resting under her raised arm; his left bent at the elbow, his hand clasping hers. Her head bent forward, finding the space between his shoulder and chin, making a shelter of him. They were together and alone, eyes nearly closed, transported. There was an erotic charge between them, but seemingly no urgency in doing anything about it. They were suspended in time, preserved in their own perfect moment of grace and surrender.

She stared at the picture wanting… what? To live inside the photo? To live in another city and live the sexy, uncomplicated life she imagined this pretty young thing in the halter-top enjoyed? It was too late now. She and Cal were in their thirties. They had dishes and furniture and a mortgage and prescriptions for anti-depressants. The time for jetting off to foreign countries was behind them. It was too late to move to Buenos Aires, to live in Parisian style walk-ups and sip cocktails with new friends from Martinique and Berlin, all driven by the same dumb-assed Bohemian fantasy.

But they could take their savings and live there for a few months. Maybe longer if they rented out their own house. She could finally work on her painting and Cal could finish his screenplay...

She reread the article and then sat for several minutes staring again at the photo. She stared at it so hard she could feel herself enter it, transported to that place of grace and calm. There was no fear there. No second thoughts. This was a real state, one she could inhabit. It had to be. She felt a sudden rush of certainty; everything would be fine, everything would work out. They just had to get to Argentina.

She put the article away and went to the kitchen where she stared out the window. The trees needed pruning. The garden was wild and untended. She unloaded the dishwasher. Cal had been gone nearly two hours already. Maybe Karin was right, they'd better find out what their next thing was if they wanted their marriage to work out, if they wanted to be happy.

She went back to the computer and started re-searching long-term rentals in Buenos Aires. She'd compiled a list of several possibilities when she realized how Cal would react; he hated change. She would have to ease him into the idea. She entered the words TANGO and PORTLAND into a search. By the time Cal returned she had signed them both up for a beginner's class at the Portland Dance Academy starting Tuesday night.

four

"GUY AT THE STORE said this harness-type collar works better. More humane," Cal explained. Rosalind watched him as he unpacked the humane collar and new leash and dog toys and chews.

"Shouldn't we be looking for the dog's owner? I was thinking of putting up some signs."

"I will," he said. "I just want him to get better first."

"First? He has owners who are probably frantic looking for him. Probably some kid."

"Yeah," he said, appraising his purchases. "I guess you're right. I'll make up some signs tomorrow."

"Don't you think we should do it today?"

"It's too soon."

"Too soon for what? He obviously has a home."

"I just — I just really want him to stay another day. I feel bad about what happened and I..." Cal stared off, tears welling in his eyes.

Rosalind reached across and took a gentle hold of Cal's hand.

"What's wrong?"

"Nothing. I just want to do the right thing. For the dog."

Rosalind studied his face carefully. He'd never been one given to easy tears. The Cal of the past few months perplexed her. She would see glimpses of her old husband, the one who knew to wrap an injured dog's snout, and then he would recede behind the veil of these strange and quick emotions. She had usually known how to read him in the past. Now he was someone to handle.

"I'm fine," he assured her, jumping forward in their stock conversation. "I'll be fine."

"You sure?" Rosalind asked, smiling hesitantly.

"Hey, buddy," he said, greeting the dog as he lifted his head, wagging his tail excitedly for Cal. Cal reached into the bag, pulling out a chew. The dog rose and then sat expectantly in front of him.

"Hey! Somebody trained you," Cal said, giving him the chew. "You still don't recognize who he looks like?"

"I still think he looks like Karl Malden. Who do you think he looks like?"

"Isn't it obvious?" Cal asked with a mixture of excitement and irritation, "He's a ringer for Jordy."

"Really? Your brother?" she asked uncertainly.

"Yeah, total dead ringer."

"I guess. I never met him so…"

"You'd see it if you had," Cal assured her handing the dog another chew.

"He thinks his brother's a dog?" asked Hermione. The sisters had arranged to meet for coffee in the late afternoon. Polly hadn't shown up yet.

"Not exactly," Rosalind protested though she was less than certain.

"How long's he been depressed?"

"A few months."

"Depression is an illness and can be treated," Hermione said with a weird, clinical delivery. "Is he taking anything?"

"Serenitol," Rosalind answered.

"Oh! That's one of ours," Hermione announced proudly. "Is it helping?"

"Actually, it's made us pretty much asexual."

"So you're not still trying to get pregnant?"

"My doctor recommended blocking off the bad tube and doing IVF which is crazy expensive. We have almost $11,000 set aside in savings, which we've talked about using, but I was depressed and then he was."

Hermione shook her head. "You can't both be depressed at the same time. That's a marriage eater!"

"Tell me about it," Rosalind sighed.

"I'm worried about you. Have you thought about an anti-depressant for yourself?"

Hermione looked genuinely concerned, but there was something about her tone that made Rosalind feel like they were starring in a pharmaceutical ad.

"I'm fine. Really. But thanks. Did you tell mom and dad about the pregnancy yet?" Rosalind asked, happy to change the subject.

"No."

"Hermione!"

"Look at the way you reacted and you're the most conventional person in the family."

"Uh, no. *You're* the most conventional person in the family now — a title I'm happy to relinquish."

"*Gaaawd*, Ros," Polly said, tossing down her backpack on the floor and settling loudly into a chair. "Could you have picked a more pretentious coffee shop?"

"You think anything nicer than *Denny's* is pretentious," Rosalind protested though, in fact, it was a very pretentious cafe. Its high ceiling, concrete floor and blond wood tables reverberated with the tapping of laptops, young moms with MFA's sharing hot chocolate with toddlers, and the upbeat chatter of web designers and urban planners. She knew it would antagonize Polly though it was hard to find much that didn't.

"How late were you guys up?" Rosalind asked.

"I haven't been to bed yet."

"Polly!"

"And Hermione went to bed right after you left," Polly told her. "You guys are getting lame in your old age. I think mom's still up making some neighbor listen to Joni Mitchell records."

Polly rose to her feet and headed to the counter, grudgingly allowing that at least the café had some vegan offerings.

"You have to tell them," Rosalind said, turning back to her conversation with Hermione.

"I don't know how. They'd be so disappointed."

"No, they won't. They love you."

"Laurent's parents have been lovely. His father built us a crib!"

"Hermione, you have to tell them."

Hermione nodded; she knew Rosalind was right.

"I'm supposed to have dinner with mom tonight. I'll tell her then."

"They're gonna wonder when you show up next year with a baby," Rosalind warned.

"I'll tell them I adopted. They'd appreciate that maybe."

Polly returned to table, sighing heavily. "So hungover." She picked at her fingernails which were, as usual, covered in patches of black or iridescent blue polish, chipped and weathered, covering only the nails' midsection. A thin blond waitress with perfect skin set a bowl of soup in front of Polly.

"Thanks," Polly said and dug in. "Gotta be in Old Town in fifteen minutes," she told them.

"Polly! I'm only here till tomorrow. At least stay a while," Hermione protested.

"I'm meeting this guy," Polly told her, as though that absolved her of any family obligations.

"What guy?" Rosalind asked.

Polly shrugged and drank her soup.

"Just this guy."

"What's his name?" Hermione asked.

"Bryan," Polly finally revealed.

"Where'd you meet him?"

"Jeez, you guys. I met him at a workshop on composting he was teaching. He's super cool. I should go," she said, reaching for her backpack, kissing both of her sisters on the cheek.

"At least finish your soup," Rosalind said.

Polly wound up her face in disgust. "They said it's vegan but there's totally cream in it. You can have it," she told them as she left.

Hermione shook her head, amused.

"I see some things never change," she said, sliding the bowl in front of her and eating. "Don't you think dying your hair pink at her age is kinda weird? She is thirty."

"You were eating out of dumpsters at thirty," Rosalind reminded her.

"It was stuff restaurants were already throwing out," Hermione explained defensively.

Rosalind shrugged. She didn't see the difference.

"What kind of dog is it?"

"What?" Rosalind asked, distracted by a toddler banging a plate at a nearby table.

"The dog Cal thinks is his brother."

"He thinks it *looks* like his brother," she corrected.

"Does it?"

"Look like Jordy?" Rosalind asked, considering the idea. "I guess a little bit."

After lunch they walked to Rosalind's store where she gave her a brief tour. Ingrid, the owner, was alone at the counter.

"Kinda slow today," she explained, unconcerned.

Ingrid was married to a Brit named Derek, which inexplicably gave her an English accent too. Their children Marthe and Augustus sometimes ran around the shop while Ingrid implored them to "give mummy a bloody break." Rosalind often helped with the bookkeeping and was well aware of the store's economic fluctuations, something that never seemed to bother Ingrid or Derek. Ingrid made a polite show of pretending to care about money every now and then — she would cut back on the nanny's hours or decide to spend only three weeks on a Greek island with the kids instead of four or, though it "really pained her" to do it, pay Rosalind fifty cents less an hour — but they were not the actions of anyone seriously worried. Rosalind could never quite figure their source of income; Derek vaguely mentioned a job in the music business that seemed to require absolutely none of his time, Ingrid had parents who "lived abroad," mentioned frequently in a tone suggesting it was code for something so delightful and rarified it was beyond Rosalind's comprehension.

Hermione ohhhed and ahhhed over all the overpriced delights of the store the way expectant mothers often did.

"Pick any piece of clothing and it's my gift to you guys," Rosalind offered.

"Are you serious?"

"Of course."

"Laurent would really get a kick out of this Sex Pistols t-shirt."

"Yeah," Rosalind said. "That's a big seller."

They hugged goodbye in front of the store. Rosalind had to run a few errands before going home.

"Good luck with mom," Rosalind said.

"Thanks. I'll need it."

"Stop by after if you want. Cal and I'll probably just be hanging out, watching a movie probably. Come for a nightcap or, y'know, a soda."

"Yeah," Hermione said, running her hands through her hair, "maybe." It was clear she wouldn't.

"Weird you're just here the weekend. Isn't it a long flight?"

"Didn't I tell you? I'm going to San Francisco for a week." She'd gone to college there and still had friends in the area. It shouldn't have stung. But it did.

"Oh," Rosalind said. "Have a great time then."

"I will."

They smiled awkwardly and hugged again. Rosalind thought briefly to ask when they'd stopped being necessary to each other, when she had become another obligation to fill like their parents or Polly.

"Have a safe flight," she told her finally.

"Thanks again for the t-shirt."

Rosalind nodded that it was nothing and then stood on the street, strangely unable to move as she watched her sister walk down the block, the brown *little fig* bag bumping against her thigh, and disappear around the corner.

five

IN THE DAYS AFTER THE accident Cal and Jordy were inseparable. They slept and ate and even worked together (Cal's office encouraged bringing dogs to work). By Tuesday it seemed to Rosalind that the dog regarded her with the wary impatience of a host whose guest had overstayed her welcome. He watched her as she moved about the house, his brown eyes never wavering. He'd raise his head expectantly whenever she got up — *oh, leaving already?* — and then lower it again with a perturbed doggy sigh when she came to rest again on the sofa or the bed. She instantly regretted allowing him into their bed, as the big brown beast seemed to grow in the night, expanding in every direction till Cal and Rosalind were clinging to the outside edges of the bed. Cal begrudged him nothing, insisting on making a homemade dog food of rice and meat he'd found a recipe for online and going for long walks.

"I forgot to mention," Rosalind began cautiously over her morning coffee — she'd not forgotten, she'd studiously avoided the subject of their future; her desire to move to Argentina in the long term and their enrollment in a beginner's tango class that evening in the short term — "we got signed up for a dance class tonight. It's at seven."

"We *got signed up*?" Cal asked, pouncing on her use of the passive voice — as though a tango class just happened to you like nearsightedness or a thunderstorm.

"I signed us up," she admitted. "It'll be fun!"

"I can't."

"How come?"

"Serious? C'mon. I can't leave Jordy alone."

"He's a dog."

"You're gonna have to cancel."

"I can't cancel! You can't just cancel a class," Rosalind said, lashing out more furiously then she'd meant to. Three sleepless nights with a giant dog and an increasingly unsteady husband was getting to her. It was so unfair. Why couldn't he just give her this one thing?

"I'm sorry," he said.

Rosalind set her coffee mug down. She wasn't going to blow up at Cal — at least not with that damned dog with his big sad brown Jordy eyes watching on.

"Fine," she said, tossing the half cup of coffee that remained and rinsing her cup under the faucet. "That's fine. Forget it."

"Plum —"

She pulled her cardigan off a hook and walked out the back door, moving quickly to her car and then waiting before starting the engine. Maybe he'd come out and apologize like he should. She looked at the door and waited. No Cal. She turned the key and started to back out the driveway when she caught sight of his brown jacket emerging from the door. Jordy followed immediately behind on his leash. It looked to her as though the dog was gloating. Cal waved a little guiltily though not enough to satisfy her as she pulled out of the driveway and headed off to work.

The morning at *little fig* was busy. There was a "mommy and me" yoga class on Tuesdays and Thursdays at the studio next door after which a rush of yoga-mommies would descend. They were thin and fit even though they talked incessantly about how motherhood had ruined their bodies. They either came from money or had married it so their days passed in, what seem to Rosalind, a languorous montage of shopping and yoga and nannies and children. One yoga mommy named Brit had bought two of Rosalind's hummingbird paintings and always treated her with an odd mixture of condescension and deference.

"This non-toxic?" Brit asked holding up a tube of sunscreen. She was tan and athletic, her hair gathered artfully in a loose topknot.

"It is. Ingrid and I both researched it," Rosalind told her.

Brit put the sunscreen on the counter along with her credit card.

"With most of these lotions we might as well spread cancer on our kids, right?" Brit said. Rosalind nodded; customers often assumed she had children too.

"We're going on vacation next week," Brit told her. The yoga-mommies were always going on vacation.

"Have a great time," Rosalind said with a clerk's smile before moving on to a yoga-mommy buying a cashmere hoodie.

Rosalind didn't have a chance to text Polly until the afternoon to see if she wanted to join her for the tango class. She had run through other possibilities, friends who might welcome the invitation, but it seemed her friends now all had small children and marriages fraught with intense, Kremlin-level negotiations regarding a night out alone. Polly was the only person she knew of with no obligations. But when she stopped by after work to pick her up she found only Helen, alone in the breakfast-nook grading papers.

"Where's Polly?"

"Think she went out with that boy. Running some sort of composting workshop," Helen said, taking Rosalind in with close scrutiny.

"Dammit."

"I objected at first but we've got a whole bin of it in the backyard and it really does make a superior mulch. Not that I care much either way but —" she sighed, "— it makes her happy."

"She was supposed to take this class with me tonight."

"What class?"

"Beginning tango."

Helen gave her a look; that was the last thing she would've guessed. Rosalind took a seat at the table and rubbed her eyes with exhaustion. How did such an unchallenging job leave her feeling so tired?

"Guess I'll just skip it," Rosalind said.

"What about Cal?"

"He was supposed to take it with me but he's coming down with a cold."

Helen nodded knowingly, taking off her glasses and setting them down with care. She gave Rosalind an anxious, maternal look. Rosalind knew the look well — she'd been giving it to Cal for months.

"How's he doing?" Helen asked.

"Fine."

"You know, your sister's very worried about you."

"Polly?"

"Course not. Hermione — in fact, you're almost all we talked about during our dinner."

"Did she say anything about herself?"

"No. We barely talked about her, come to think of it. Guess she and Anton are working on a production of *Mother Courage*."

"Uh huh."

Rosalind rose to get herself a glass of water. She stood at the sink, drinking her water, and watched the sun breaking through the fir trees in the backyard. She fantasized about sleeping for a year or two and waking when this rough patch of life was over, when normalcy was restored.

Helen pushed aside her glasses and papers, placing her palms flat on the table as though absorbing an insight so powerful she needed to steady herself.

"Why don't I go with you?"

"Where?" Rosalind asked.

"Your tango class."

"Oh, yeah —" Rosalind froze in panic. "I don't know if you'd like it. Tango is highly gendered."

Helen dismissed this with a wave.

"All the better. It'll be like anthropological research then."

"I don't think I want to go," Rosalind said. She couldn't imagine anything worse than a tango class with her mother.

"I'll go with you this week and next week when Cal's better he can take you."

"I don't know," Rosalind said. "It's a really bad cold. I'll just see if I can get a refund."

"To hell with that! We're going to tango."

Rosalind took a deep breath and felt dread tightening her gut as Helen poured the remnants of her tea down the sink. They were going.

six

THE FIRST THING ROSALIND NOTICED was the shoes. It was a beginner's class yet everyone (excluding Rosalind and Helen, of course) seemed to have shoes for the occasion. Many of the women had remarkable shoes, as though they signed up for the class just to wear them. The shoes ran the gamut: strappy, high-heeled, open-toed, covered, round-toed, pointy. One pair looked like it had been dipped in the shimmery gold powder used to kill off a Bond girl.

Rosalind was lost in a sea of sexy shoes. She suddenly wished she had worn her one pair of sexy high heels, the ones she wore when she knew she'd be sitting most of the night. Instead she wore her everyday summer sandals, the ones she wore to work — a bit of a heel, comfortable and worn in, shabby now that she saw them in the harsh light of the dance studio next to all the glamour heels. On closer inspection *she* was shabby too. The room was a long rectangle with mirrors spanning one wall. It was used for all kinds of dance classes but a couple of posters filled the blank patches of wall showing couples in various tango poses.

The class was larger than Rosalind had expected, maybe forty people, and was filled with such a diverse assortment of ages and ethnicities that it reminded her of jury duty. The room had a restive air as people chatted, waiting for the instructors to show. There were couples and singles — a few women, the most dolled up actually, were there with their gay best friends.

Rosalind stared at the door wishing she hadn't come: trying new things was stupid. What was wrong with drinking a couple of glasses of wine, crawling into bed early and having a good cry like she usually did? She looked at her mother who was awkwardly shifting her weight from one foot to another. This was a terrible idea! Maybe it wasn't too late to talk Helen into doing something else. Just as Rosalind moved towards Helen, devising a plan, the instructors arrived. Barry and Mariela Pierson took their place at the front of the class, commanding in attitude but far from Rosalind's expectations. She hadn't realized it until this moment but she'd come expecting an Argentine stereotype to lead the class: a sassy Latina or an old man from the *barrio* who, in spite of his bawdy jokes, was courtly with the ladies and dispensed cryptic life lessons between choreography. Barry and Mariela were white and in their mid-forties and had had a twenty-plus-year long "affair with the Argentine tango," they explained, and though they originally hailed from Boulder, Colorado, they had traveled often, sometimes for extended stays, to Argentina to study with its greatest teachers and dance in its most famous *milongas*.

Barry was large and bulky — a figure more likely to be found in a log-splitting contest than a Argentine *milonga* — wearing a black dress shirt and jeans. His wife, Mariela (she had been Mary Ellen before the affair with Argentina began) looked more like a dancer though she seemed to strain for this effect; her hair was pulled back stylishly in a French knot and she wore a black slit skirt, a fitted red shirt with a little ballerina's shrug pulled over it. They looked like the optimistic, tightly bonded couple who led weekend retreats for couples trying to restore "magic and fire" to their relationship — in fact, there were even flyers for an upcoming retreat in September in the lobby, Mariela told them.

"OK! Let's get started," Mariela announced brightly. "Now, can anyone tell me the meaning of 'tango' — the actual word?"

Helen, of course, knew. "In Latin it means 'I touch.'"

Mariela nodded emphatically. "'I touch.' Or 'I play.' As in playing an instrument only here our instrument is *ourselves*," Mariela paused, allowing this insight to sink in. "And it means 'I touch. I touch my partner in embrace,'" Dan and Mariela faced each other in an opening stance, "also called an *abrazo* —" and danced a simple eight step.

"And I touch my inner life. I touch the core of my essence. Tango is not just learning or following steps."

"It's improvisation," Barry said in a deep baritone.

"That's right. There's a saying that tango is a 'sad thought danced.' But that's only part of it. It's touching the sadness in you, the pain, yes — but also the joy, the humor, the everything life has. It's touching everything."

"Touching everything," Barry happily agreed.

Barry and Mariela divided the room into men and women.

"Ladies, follow me," Mariela told them, leading them to one side of the room. The "gentlemen" took the other side of the room with Barry.

"Now, ladies, remember the feet stay close to the ground in tango. As if you are sliding a piece of paper with the bottom of your foot."

She showed them the eight step she had just performed with Barry. The movements were simple, elegant but for the twenty women staring uncomfortably at their full-length reflections in the mirror, it was another matter. Rosalind found she took to the steps more easily than she would've guessed but Helen struggled. She wasn't used to much physical activity anymore and her legs moved laboriously underneath her, she took large, distinct steps, in contrast to the easy gliding pattern Mariela showed her. Rosalind felt a teenaged mortification; her mother was so embarrassing: overweight, clumsy and awkward. Rosalind regretted bringing her here, she regretted signing up for the class, she regretted the invention of the Internet that allowed bad decisions like this one to be made so quickly and conveniently.

"Keep your feet close to the floor but then also lift up from your flower," Mariela told her, drawing a sweeping line with her hand from her lower abdomen up through her head.

"My what?" asked Helen.

Oh no, thought Rosalind. This was precisely why she didn't want Helen to come, why she'd invited even Polly, of all people, before thinking to invite Helen — even though Polly would have certainly found a way to interpret the tango as classist or racist or somehow contributing to greenhouse gases.

"Your flower," Mariela repeated.

"Do you mean my *vagina*?" Helen asked, matter of fact.

"Well…"

"I am a sixty seven year old woman," she explained calmly as if lecturing an undergraduate, "I have a vagina. Not a flower. Not a lotus. Not a vajayjay or any other cutesy icky-poo names you want to come up with.

I have a vagina. If that's what you're referencing, please call it that."

Mariela studied her with a look of profound confusion. Some of the women giggled in discomfort.

"Or vulva, if that makes you more comfortable," Helen generously allowed. This did not seem to make Mariela more comfortable.

"I meant, actually," Mariela said, gathering her bearings — she wasn't going to be pushed around in her own class, "everything. Your head, your mind, your sensuality. Your sensuality isn't just your vagina."

"Agreed."

"It's your totality. Your whole woman-ness, your essential woman-ness."

Rosalind's heart sank. Not essentialism! The very concept was Helen's bête noire, she had whole set speeches built around the subject, describing in excruciating detail how men and women biologically were more similar than dissimilar; how for all the foofaraw about "Mars" and "Venus" brains there was very little research showing much difference aside from a larger corpus callosum in women and greater lateralization of function; how the differences between men and women were not primal or basic or conclusive, but in fact a mystification that enabled the subjugation of one half of the population politically, socially, and economically to the other for thousands of years, and existed in today's popular culture as a marketing ploy to sell douches, beer, engagement rings, sporting events, cars, romance novels, self-help books and magazine subscriptions in a network so vast and unquestioned in its primacy she dubbed it the "sexual difference industrial complex."

Rosalind stared down at the floor, shaking her head. Helen looked at Rosalind and seemed to remember why she'd come in the first place.

"I don't typically subscribe to notions of essential sex differences, in fact, I see difference as more of a spectrum —" Helen began, then seeing again Rosalind's worried look, "— but for the purposes of this class we can provisionally interrogate the notion."

The class returned to the basic step. Side, back, back, cross, back, side, together. It seemed simple enough until you had to remember it. Add music and a partner and the task quickly seemed insurmountable. Barry explained about the line of dance, how couples were meant to move in a counter-clockwise circle. Men led, women followed. Men directed the flow of traffic, they looked out for their partners. Women, from what Rosalind could gather, were always dancing backwards and relied on the men to steer them safely among the other couples. In advanced stages, Mariela explained, women are known to dance with their eyes closed. They were literally dancing blind. Already Rosalind was confronted with her two least favorite things: full-length mirrors and relying on a partner to stay out of trouble.

Barry told them to couple up, gentleman ask the lady for a dance — Rosalind watched her mother as a flicker of disgust registered on her face and then dissipated; she really was making an effort. A pleasant young man who introduced himself as Ben asked Rosalind to dance and she watched, smiling to herself, as an elfin man in his fifties bowed politely to Helen, offering his hand. The music began. Couples assumed the "practice embrace" with hands held loosely on a partner's upper arms. And everybody moved — quickly, then slowly, then haltingly — into each other.

Couples clustered in great chunks at the end of the imaginary circle, more of a scattered rhombus of collisions than a line of dance. Rosalind danced with a series of gray-faced bachelors in khaki pants, occasionally sitting a dance out; there were a few more women than men and even though they were all exhorted to switch partners, the wives held greedily onto their husbands for the most part. Had it not been for the scattering of anxious bachelors and over-dressed women with gay best friends who'd clearly both come boyfriend shopping, there'd be no switching at all.

The men were often mischievous, enjoying their power; the women couldn't make a move unless they did. At least three men Rosalind danced with caught her moving forward without them — she was still preoccupied with getting the steps right and would barrel forward in her enthusiasm at actually remembering what to do. They would smile, a glint. She'd been naughty, not waiting. *Now* you can move. And now again. And…not now. Caught you! This went on all night. With some men it was funny and charming and with others faintly menacing. She was overstepping their control. Move…now! It was revealing being this close to a stranger and getting such a strong dose of his personality. Within seconds she felt she could read a man's need to dominate, accommodate or befriend a woman. This impression was so strong she wondered what these strangers were able to read from her.

"Hi, I'm Bobby," a man in his thirties told her. Bobby was a tall black man with loose, short dreads and an easy smile.

"Hi. Rosalind."

"Nice to meet you, Rosalind."

They began the step and Rosalind noticed immediately the difference of dancing with someone who actually knew how to lead. The steps came easily. There was no stumbling or giggles or apologies.

"What other dance classes have you taken?" Bobby asked.

"Me? None. Well, some cheesy jazz stuff when I was a kid."

"Really? You're really good!"

"I am?"

"Yeah, really good."

"Thanks. You too."

The dance ended and Bobby thanked her. "Save another one for me," he told her with a wink before turning to an older woman with brightly-dyed red hair. Rosalind wanted him back, wanted to spend the whole night just practicing the same little eight steps over and over. She was embarrassed to think how much. It was intoxicating being this close to a succession of men, all closely focused on her, on her movements. She realized how invisible she felt living with Cal.

She moved mechanically through the steps with a Russian man in his sixties loudly chewing Chiclets. He liked to play gotcha: *step, step, wait! I didn't move...and move now.* Bobby didn't play that game, Rosalind remembered, already nostalgic about their dance. She noticed her mother struggling gamely through the steps, grimly apoplectic with these men and their stupid games and this silly over-gendered dance. And then the music ended.

"Good work, everyone," Barry told them. "See you back here next week."

Rosalind caught her mother making a "yeah, right" gesture with her head as they both moved to the corner to gather their things.

"I'm sure you and Cal will have a lot of fun with the class," Helen diplomatically summed up on the way home in the car.

"I told you you wouldn't like it."

"I know but I didn't want you going alone," Helen huffed.

"Yeah, because I might enjoy myself and not be humiliated."

"Humiliated?"

"Mom, who cares if she wants to call her vagina a flower. Who the hell cares? It's hers, she can call it what she likes."

"You made my point exactly. *Her* vagina. Not *mine*. She was talking about mine. Oh God, and that shit about essential woman-ness."

"It's her class," Rosalind reminded her. "Who's she hurting?"

"She's a teacher. She's spreading wrong thinking."

"*Wrong thinking?* Who are you, the *politburo?*"

"I think she should consider her words more carefully."

"OK, well, it's a moot point anyway cause that was your last class."

"Agreed," Helen nodded. They'd finally arrived at the house and Helen grabbed her purse. "I just didn't want you going alone."

"Mom, I appreciate your concern but I'm fine. Cal's fine. We're all fine," Rosalind assured her.

"OK. You wanna come in for a glass of wine?"

"No, thanks. I'm tired. Goodnight."

Helen made her way up the stairs as Rosalind put the car into gear and headed home. She hadn't traced the route from her parents' home to her own since the night of the unniversary party and had a sinking feeling as she grew closer to the spot. She slowed down, inspecting the telephone poles, the naked telephone poles unspoiled by the signs Cal swore he'd put up.

She had to pull over because she couldn't see anymore. Her heart pounded, she felt suddenly ill. She filled her lungs with air, trying to calm herself but it was no use. Cal had lied to her. He never lied. Or did he? She was furious and hurt. She started the car up again and raced all the way home.

seven

ROSALIND COULD HEAR VOICES, her rage rising as she turned the key: Glen was over. She found the men in their usual seats, an empty pizza container, *Kill Bill Volume II* playing on the TV with the sound off and Jimi Hendrix playing on the stereo. The dog slept peacefully at the edge of the sofa, waking with Rosalind's entrance, registering it with one of his irritated sighs before harrumphing his snout under one of his great paws.

"Hey," Cal said with a sleepy smile. "Where you been? I was worried."

"I can see," Rosalind said, taking in the state of the room.

"Y'know who's overrated? Shakespeare," Glen thought out loud, "I mean, are his plays really that good? I never thought so."

"Don't say that to Plum's mom — she teaches that," Cal warned.

"No kidding?"

"Her specialty is English theatre before the Restoration when men played all the parts. It's a whole gender as performance thing," Rosalind told him mechanically as she stared at Cal in disbelief.

"Where were you?" he asked.

"I went to that dance class."

"Oh, yeah. You like it?"

"I noticed on the way home someone tore down your signs," Rosalind said.

"What signs?"

"The signs for the dog?"

"Oh, yeah," he said as if only just recalling the large dog sleeping next to him. "I actually didn't get to them yet."

"Cal…" Rosalind said, her voice laced with weary disappointment. "*You told me you did.*"

"I said I was *going to*, I didn't say I *had*."

"Actually, you did," she corrected him.

"We've been watching *The Wire*," Glen offered, as though that absolved Cal.

"I don't care," Rosalind snapped.

Glen shrugged and picked up a magazine, leafing through it, his head shaking back and forth in tight, small movements in time with a guitar solo. He'd grown used to these disagreements between Cal and Rosalind.

"Thing is," Cal admitted, "he's been limping a bit and I wanted to take him to Tobin's vet. Says he's great." An expensive vet, no doubt — Tobin always insisted on the very best. Tobin was Cal's boss, the owner of *DimeEdge*. Like Cal, Tobin had been raised in affluence, fell into an immediately successful company and therefore had a fundamental inability to understand anyone who couldn't easily land a high-paying job or pay top dollar for anything he needed.

"How much is it going to cost?" Rosalind asked.

Cal raised an eyebrow in disapproval. He brought home the bulk of the money in their household and while he was normally affable enough about the fact, he didn't like to be challenged about how he spent money.

"He said it's kind of a miracle the dog walked away from that accident. A miracle."

"You already went?" Rosalind asked, surprised.

"Yeah, he had a spot open this afternoon and Tobin says he's super hard to get into so, anyway, this guy says Jordy's definitely gonna need knee surgery down the line though. Guess that other vet was right. ACL's on both hind legs are going."

"How much did he charge?"

"Said the surgery could run up to seven, eight grand for both knees."

"How much was the visit?"

Cal shrugged. "A few hundred."

"Cal! We're already a few hundred in from the first guy!"

"Don't worry about it."

"Telling me not to worry doesn't make me not worry," she said.

"Right. I'm goin'," Glen announced.

"You going to the Astor?" Cal asked. Astor was his favorite bar — or had been — Glen gave a look of disgust.

"Naw. Full of fuckers in porkpie hats now. See ya guys."

"Bye," Rosalind said, closing the door behind him and then turning to Cal with a look.

"Don't worry," Cal told her irritably. "I mean — it is my money."

"Your money?"

"I didn't mean it like that —"

She turned for the bedroom, shutting the door behind her.

"Hey. Plum?" Cal knocked softly on the door. "I'm sorry. I'm really sorry. I didn't mean it like that."

Rosalind sat on the bed staring at the collection of dog toys on the floor. Cal opened the door and sat down next to her, taking her hand in his. The dog's paws click-clicked in a slow, late night rhythm until he hopped up on the bed with them, making himself comfortable dead center.

"You know, you're not supposed to let dogs sleep in your bed. It sends the wrong message. They're supposed to see you as dominant," she told Cal.

"Huh," Cal snorted thoughtfully.

The dog nudged his bottom into Rosalind, his tail flopping huffily on her hip.

"What I'm saying is, that dog needs to sleep on the goddamn floor, Cal."

"OK, OK. C'mon, pal," he coaxed him with a cheerful voice. The dog hopped down, ever compliant where Cal was concerned, and planted himself on the floor next to him.

"Plum?" he asked stroking her hand gently.

"Yeah?"

"Why did you sign us up for a tango class?"

"I thought it would be fun," she said. It wasn't the whole truth but it sounded less crazy than wanting to live inside a photograph.

"Was it?"

She longed to tell him it was, that it was just the thing to get their marriage back on track. But she couldn't lie.

"Not really. I went with mom."

Cal laughed loudly and she joined him.

"I also — I heard Argentina's sort of the place to be. Like it's cheap and artistic and there's lots of cool restaurants and Cal, we could live there for not much money. We could live there for a few months on our savings, longer if we rent out this place. You could write your script and I could paint."

"I can write here. You can paint here," he told her.

"We could but we don't."

"Why would we there?"

"Because. We'd be awake. We'd be doing something different and I think it would just wake us up. Or me anyway. I feel so tired all the time. I'm just in this fog and I feel so unproductive and uncreative and just... boring."

"What're we gonna live on?"

"Our savings."

"The baby money?" he asked, incredulous.

"We're never called it that before," she protested, as if that made her plan any more realistic. "I feel like if things were better it'd just happen. Y'know we'd get into this creative place and we wouldn't need all these *chemicals* to regulate our moods or be happy or make a baby."

There was a long silence.

"I don't know. Doesn't sound like a good idea," he said, standing and undressing.

Rosalind stared at him.

"What?" he asked.

"Just like that?" she asked, her face flush. Was she actually about to cry? She hadn't realized how much this fantasy had come to mean to her. All this deliberation and when she finally said it out loud it all made sense. *They had to go.* It was their last hope.

Cal sat down next to her in boxers and socks.

"Plum, don't cry. We'll talk about it, OK? I want to hear about it. Just not tonight, I'm so tired."

"This is important to me," she told him.

"I see that. And we'll talk about it, I promise."

She nodded and let him hug her as they both, exhausted and teary, drifted off to sleep.

Rosalind felt a hot, foul breath on her and turned to see the dog had climbed quietly up and onto the center of the bed again. She was too tired to resist and fell into an exhausted half sleep interrupted, she wasn't sure how much later — was it minutes or hours? — by the dog whose back paws had shoved her to the edge of the bed. In her half-sleep state she clung to the sheet and then awoke completely, in time to watch the dog raise his head and fix her with his complacent gaze and with a little shove of his back leg push her out of the bed entirely.

That was it. That was it! That was fucking it. Rosalind wasn't even going to wake Cal and rationally discuss the damn dog anymore. He couldn't be trusted where that dog was concerned. She pulled herself up from the floor, glaring at the dog as she went into the tiny office off the kitchen and turned on the computer. She found what she needed; there were already several photos of the dog uploaded to the computer and in fact, it appeared a calendar of sorts was in the works. She made up a sign with a picture and the headline: HAVE YOU LOST ME?

She gave her cell phone as a contact; she didn't trust Cal to take the call.

It was five in the morning. The air was crisp and a few birds chirped intermittently. Rosalind steered through empty streets, encountering, even at that hour, a few joggers already out. She took the signs and posted them to the telephone poles, their surfaces usually already covered in staples. She wrapped the signs in great wide strips of packing tape, the silence of dawn broken by her tape dispenser. By the tenth corner she finally started running low on signs. She ran out of tape first and tossed the rest of the signs in her front seat. She sat at the wheel of her car, exhaling softly as the sun lightened the blue sky and crows conversed from the treetops. It was lovely out. It was going to be a beautiful day. She turned on the engine and headed home.

By the time she got home she was too tired to sleep. It was six and too late to really get any sleep anyway. She decided to go for a run. She hadn't gone for a run since before the pregnancy, she realized, lacing up her shoes. Madly posting signs in the early morning reminded her how much she liked this time. She'd grown used to sleeping in, hastily racing through preparations for work and then sitting on a stool for eight hours, leaving her drained and exhausted. It was an exhaustion she didn't feel entitled to. She wished at times she were engaged in some great physical labor to justify such profound tiredness — or at least a job in which lives were marginally better at the end of her shift. She'd fallen into working at *little fig*. It was supposed to be temporary, meant to bring in some cash while she looked for a "real job" many years ago.

The tango class, the whiff of dawn air — both reminded her that she at least had a body, one she'd been neglecting. She ran at a faster pace than she was used to and quickly grew a side-ache. She was out of shape and took long, heaving breaths as she strode quickly to the park where she liked to run the perimeter. Life was busy at this hour: commuters and children and joggers and bikers. There was a whole world outside her home and her work; she'd forgotten how much. She walked most of the way back, stopping occasionally to crane back and adjust a knot in her upper back or shoulder.

Boring jobs were murder on the back. She should really get back to yoga someday. She walked up the steps to their house, noting the geraniums in clay pots that needed deadheading. Maybe that would be her new routine: running and then gardening. It would be her own local version of who she imagined she'd become in Argentina.

She chucked her keys in the basket at the front door, noticing her cell phone.

"Hi," a polite male voice said on her voicemail, "this is Eric Ames. I think you have my dog."

eight

Rosalind hadn't expected someone to call about the dog so soon. In her fit of pique she'd somehow lost sight of the fact that someone would call at all. She hadn't told Cal yet. By the afternoon she'd decided they were both being silly. It was just a dog. A dog that probably belonged to Eric Ames who would be very grateful when they called. He might offer them a reward and they would nobly refuse. It was an everyday event: dog lost, dog found. Dog returns home. Only bad people didn't return dogs, sick people, poor citizens.

Rosalind dialed. She left a brief message on his voicemail and then prayed some customers would come in to occupy her mind. The dog deliberations were consuming her. It couldn't be healthy.

Rosalind's cell phone rang almost instantly. It was her mother.

"Hi, Mom—"

"I've been researching the etymology," her mother began without a greeting, as she usually did when something was on her mind.

"Of what?"

"*Tango*. That woman's completely wrong. It has nothing to do with Latin."

"This isn't a good —"

"There's some disagreement, but it most likely means closed space or a circle. In fact during slave trading 'tango' was where slaves were kept. It's supposed to mean black people dancing — the dance derived from blacks in South America."

"Mom—"

"Typical. It's always about Europe."

This seemed a little rich coming from a Shakespeare scholar but Rosalind didn't feel like getting into it.

"Any case, I definitely want to go with you to class next week and straighten that lady out."

"Mom, you're not coming. I don't want another scene."

"I didn't make a scene."

Rosalind had another call coming in: Eric Ames.

"I'm gonna have to call you back."

Rosalind hesitated. In the few hours since he'd entered their lives, Eric Ames had taken on a near mythical potency. What would Cal do when she told him Jordy had been claimed?

"Hello?"

"Hi. Eric Ames. Thanks so much for your sign. You can imagine I was pretty worried."

"Yeah."

"How's he doing?"

"He's fine. Fine," she told him.

"Great. Where do you live? I can come over tonight."

"Oh. Yeah, we're in Southeast but maybe — I don't know if tonight's going to work — we have plans," she lied. She worried now what the dog's loss would do to Cal.

"Tomorrow morning? I teach so I'm up pretty early. Would that be alright?"

"Yeah... that's fine."

There was an uncomfortably long silence that Eric Ames finally broke.

"Is everything OK?"

She knew he was asking about the dog but she still had to suppress an urge to tell him all that was on her mind.

"Actually there was an accident — that's how we found him — but he's fine now. We took him to the vet. Two vets. Clean bill of health."

"Oh, good. I've had problems with him getting out — he's so good at it. I guess you've noticed."

"No, actually he's been very well behaved."

Eric Ames laughed. "Maybe he belongs to you guys."

Rosalind didn't want to tell him how much. She joined in the laughter half-heartedly.

They arranged for him to pick the dog up the following evening.

She waited until after dinner to tell Cal, after they'd eaten their rotisserie chicken in front of the TV and quietly scraped the bones into the trash, Cal setting aside some dark meat for the dog.

"I heard from his owner," Rosalind said casually, rinsing the plate before setting it in the dishwasher.

"You what?" Cal asked, kneeling down to give the dog some chicken.

"Yeah. He called me."

"How'd he find you?"

"I put up some signs when I noticed there weren't any," she said.

"When?"

"Last night. When I dropped mom off. I saw there weren't any signs and I figured someone'd torn them down," she didn't like to lie — she knew it was a slippery slope in a relationship but he was the one who'd started with the lying and besides she wasn't ready to tell the four a.m. story. It made her seem as crazy as she felt.

"I don't understand," he said. "You saw the signs weren't there and you went back to your folks' house to make signs?"

"Yeah."

"Or you just made them on the spot?"

"What does it matter? He called, I called him back. It's his dog."

"Why didn't you tell me last night then?"

"Tell you what?"

"That you'd put up signs."

"Oh my God," she groaned. "Who cares?"

"I care."

"It's not your dog, Cal. It's not your dog and it's not your brother. It's a dog that belongs to Eric Ames."

"Who is this guy? What do we know about him?"

"We know he's the guy who owns this dog," she told him, trying to control her irritation.

"How do we know for sure?"

"He saw the picture."

Cal nodded, briefly satisfied by this. "How'd you have a picture?"

And so it all came out: how Rosalind had been shoved out of the bed, how she'd come to make signs at four in the morning and then tape them to telephone poles and then went for a jog, realizing how narrow her life had become and how much they needed to go to Argentina. Cal sat down and nodded calmly like a veteran cop processing the details of a grisly murder; none of it seemed to throw him, nothing upset him. He just listened and nodded and then stared thoughtfully out the window.

"Well," he said finally, "you're just gonna have to tell him we don't have the dog."

Rosalind laughed, pleased that he was able to joke about it. But he didn't laugh.

"Jesus, Cal, you're not — we're not people that don't return dogs. That's just weird."

"Here's the thing: the way you talk about Argentina is what Jordy gives me. If you can have Argentina why can't I have the dog?"

"First of all, nobody *owns* Argentina so it's not like I'm depriving someone of something that's rightfully theirs and second, according to you last night, I don't get Argentina. You totally shot it down."

Cal nodded and frowned in the way he did when he was about to bring up something he didn't want to bring up.

"It's just I'm wondering if Argentina isn't just like when you decided you had to reorganize the house and kept buying and returning all those bins at Target," he said. "You get on these obsessions thinking they'll fix everything. They won't. It's magical thinking."

"Magical thinking? You think your brother's come back as a dog," Rosalind shot back. From his wounded look she could tell she'd gone a bit too far. "What I'm worried about," she began hesitantly, "is who you think the dog is."

"What?"

"Do you think the dog looks like Jordy or *is* Jordy?"

Cal put his face in his hands and breathed deeply.

"I'm not gonna get into that," he told her and promptly rose from the table, grabbing the dog's leash. "We're going for a walk."

"Would you like me to come?" she offered. She tried not to sound worried.

"No. We'll go alone. When's this guy supposed to pick him up?"

"Tomorrow."

Cal took this in, again nodding soberly and then quietly excusing himself with the dog.

Dog and man slept soundly that night — he didn't usurp Rosalind's place but seemed to match Cal's mood of sad resignation. When the time arrived Cal and the dog were ready, calmly watching television when Eric Ames showed up precisely at the appointed time. Rosalind escorted him into the living room.

"Hey, Prince. Here, boy!"

The dog regarded him skeptically before rising unsteadily to his feet and moving to sniff him. Eric bent over, stroking the dog cheerfully — he had, strangely for the season, a light raincoat over his teacher's uniform of khakis and white buttoned-down shirt. He was tall and lanky and pale with fingertips blackened, he explained, from days in front of a dry erase board explaining algebra to high-schoolers. He looked tired but moved with a kind of easy deliberateness.

"Prince?" Cal asked. He clearly didn't approve of the name.

Eric shrugged.

"My wife's idea. She thinks Prince's the greatest musician ever." Eric gave another shrug to indicate he wasn't entirely convinced of this but it wasn't anything he was going to pick a fight over.

"I'm sure your wife will be happy to see him again," Rosalind said, trying to reinforce for Cal what a good thing they were doing.

"Divorced," Eric said and then held up his bare ring finger as if to prove it.

"Oh. I'm sorry," she said.

"You know, we actually had kind of a little custody battle over Prince which she finally won. Next thing I know she's moved into this condo with her new boyfriend that doesn't allow pets and suddenly she doesn't care. The dog's back to me." Eric gave a grim little laugh at the irony of it all.

"We've really enjoyed him and I'm glad you've got him back," she said diplomatically.

"Why didn't you put up signs?" Cal asked. Prince had finished sniffing Eric and returned to his spot sleeping at Cal's feet.

"Sorry?"

"You could've put up signs yourself but you didn't."

"I put a post up on Craigslist. I thought that's what people do nowadays," Eric explained.

"No, they put up signs," Cal told him.

"I'm sorry — am I? —" Eric looked to Rosalind for translation, sensing she was his ally in this.

"Cal really loves your dog is all. OK! It was really nice to meet you and good luck with your dog and everything," she said, trying to walk Eric and Prince to the door. But Cal rose to his feet, one final question from the prosecution.

"Why was he out? At that hour?"

"I told you," Rosalind said sharply. "He gets out."

"Never got out from me," Cal said.

"I'd love to hear how you did that sometime," Eric told him, surprisingly good humored about the whole thing — years spent teaching math to teenagers, Rosalind speculated, had made him unflappable.

"Thanks for taking such good care of him," Eric said as he pulled out Prince's leash. Rosalind could see Cal trying to restrain himself but he couldn't. He went to the kitchen, grabbing the leash he'd bought, the toys, the treats, lovingly placing them in a plastic sack for them to take home. Eric appreciatively took the newer, better leash, assuring Cal he would use it instead from now on.

"C'n I see him? Y'know, visit?" Cal asked plaintively. It broke Rosalind's heart.

Eric smiled uncertainly, thrown by the oddness of the request.

"Sure."

They stood side by side and watched as Jordy/Prince hopped into the back seat of Eric Ames's red Subaru Forrester and turned to face them — staring at them, Cal really —through the car's window. Rosalind felt a perplexing sense of loss, a milestone being passed, as though Cal and she were watching their youngest drive off to college. She reached out and found his hand. He let her. They stood like that even after the car had driven off, quietly confused by the emotions surging through them. The unclasping of hands would acknowledge that they had been clasped in the first place. Over a dog. A dog that wasn't even theirs. Cal pulled his hand away first. Rosalind looked at him lovingly.

She studied him, remembering the night it felt like it all started, Cal's descent. They had gone out to dinner ostensibly, again, to cheer up Rosalind. It was a new Indian fusion restaurant, trendy with a dimly lit bar with concrete floors and low, stuffed booths in reds and purples while old Bollywood musicals played on flat-screen TV's mounted overhead. The restaurant had its own cocktail "program" because every place in Portland did. Cal had ordered something with ginger and lime and scotch. He lifted his glass in a toast but water had condensed on the sides making the glass slippery and the whole thing slid right through his hand landing at his feet where it crashed loudly on the concrete. Cal stared at his hand with a look of utter desolation as if he couldn't believe it; one more thing had slipped through his fingers. The waitress hastily replaced the drink and Cal made a show of not minding but Rosalind could tell something had shifted.

"I'm really sorry about the dog," she said and for a brief flicker she saw the old Cal. He smiled a sad smile and then the veil came down again and he shrugged and walked to the couch, flipping on the TV with the remote.

"Do you want to talk?" Rosalind asked, hoping to recall that little flicker. He shook his head, not looking up from the TV where he scanned robotically through channels.

"Cal?"

He shook his head once more. "I'm fine," he said flatly.

She could tell she'd lost him again.

nine

ROSALIND WENT TO THE SECOND tango class alone. She wore her same old, crappy sandals and this time didn't really care. It had been a long week of politeness and silence between her and Cal. He had begun to find reasons to stay late at work and Rosalind took the early evenings to go out for a run, even on the nights she was tired from another day of *little fig*. The class warmed up for the first ten minutes, reviewing the eight simple steps they'd learned last week. She hadn't practiced the steps since their last class but was surprised to realize her feet remembered them without much effort. There was something relaxing about the repetition; it took just enough effort to occupy her mind but not so much as to tax it. She danced with Larry, a middle aged realtor from Beaverton. Larry didn't play the gotcha game which pleased Rosalind. Just over and over, round the counter clockwise line of dance, the same eight steps: side, back, back, cross, back, side, together. Over and over again.

She occasionally looked over at Larry, still unsure where one was politely supposed to look during the dance. They had only been instructed not to look at their feet. The music, a plaintive, wailing song of love and loss — she knew just enough Spanish to make out that much — played loudly. She closed her eyes briefly and imagined herself in Argentina with everything in her life magically fixed. Larry stepped on her toe.

"Sorry."

"No, it's my fault," she said, noticing over the tip of Larry's shoulder a horrifying sight: her mother had come to tango class. There was a rustle of energy as others noticed her entrance, sharing amused smiles; it was going to be an interesting class. The song ended and Barry and Mariela took their places at the front. Helen found Rosalind and moved to stand next to her.

"I won't embarrass you," Helen leaned over and said softly.

I won't embarrass you. Helen had said this with such frequency and with such a total lack of accuracy over the years that the Plumley girls had made a joke of it; it was what they said to one another right before they did something potentially mortifying. Barry split the class into men and women again, Mariela casting a wary glance at Helen to see if this would cause any trouble. Tonight they learned *ochoes*, a figure eight-like step on alternating feet. Once again, it seemed simple, beautiful, effortless when Barry and Mariela demonstrated it but once the movements were broken down they seemed impossibly difficult.

"Step right and then left and *ocho* and *ocho* and *ocho*. Lovely, ladies. Again."

"How do we know if we're supposed to go into the *ocho*?" one of the women asked.

"The man will guide you," Mariela said. "He'll turn his upper body and yours will follow."

The music began. "Practice embrace" — Rosalind's new favorite phrase. She noticed her partner, one of the men who'd so playfully enjoyed his power last week now looked confused, his confidence dissolved. The introduction of *ochoes* was like a stink bomb of anxiety thrown squarely into the center of class. Men now looked hopelessly across the abyss separating their bodies from the women. There were telepathic pleas for help. What's next? That's right! Shoulders! The upper body had been introduced and they all wilted before its complex demands. Upper and lower body both doing stuff? At the same time? Too much!

There was stumbling and laughter and a few rare moments in which the steps were remembered by both parties at the same time, causing brief spells of pleasure interrupted by the realization that they had to do it all over again — were in fact in the middle of doing it all over again — and had forgotten everything, their feet lost, the steps disappearing underneath them as mysteriously as they'd once appeared. The line of dance resembled a drunken ant farm, nobody even bothered to apologize when they bumped into each other it happened so often. Rosalind was dancing with one of the gay best friends, a handsome, heavily scented young man named Kev. He announced at the start that he liked to dance as quickly as possible and, true to his word, guided her at breakneck speed, barely pausing for her *ocho*, forcing her to whip from one side to another, turning violently and inexpertly from her hip in a way she could tell she'd pay for in the morning. Kev thought this was all mad fun as he indifferently banged them into one irritated, lumbering couple after another.

"Why be slow?" he asked, delighted with his policy. Kev thought he was a real stitch. Rosalind smiled as though this was her idea of fun too, but really Kev was a pain.

"It's like weaving in and out of traffic!" he said, whipping her around one last time. Rosalind smiled politely even though she hated weavers so much that some afternoons in traffic she had to restrain herself from honking at them and yelling out her window what a rude and dangerous mess they made of the road. The music ended and he thanked her. She looked over to see Helen had been dancing with Andrew, one of the other gay best friends. The class took a break during which Helen regaled Rosalind with her latest breakthrough: tango was fascinating.

"It's all about foregrounding the constructedness of gender!" she enthused. "I don't know how I could've been so dismissive. Well, I didn't know!"

This was the charming contradiction of Helen: she was stubborn and adamant but just as available to admitting she was wrong, diving headlong into some new obsession. And her curiosity was infectious. Already she had managed to befriend the gay best friends, who had all found one another, swapping Marlboro Ultra Lights in the studio's entrance during breaks. She had told them how tango very likely came over from Africa in a direct line to the social dances that regulated courtship, power, and rites of passage. It was a dance of black people and then later the Argentine working class and laborers. It was a dance between men originally — there were no women working the fields of the Pampas. And then when women were introduced it was only prostitutes. Respectable women of Argentina did not dance the tango. Not until it had been popularized in the salons of Paris before World War I and, in a curious instance of a European colonizing nation co-opting then legitimizing a nation's dance and feeding it back to them, made socially acceptable. The highly gendered dance that typified modern tango was indeed a modern phenomenon, one that highlighted with zoot suits and slit skirts the artificial nature of its intensely coded gender roles.

This was how it always was with Helen: she went from annoying agitator to beloved star. She fell in love with her subjects and her passions ignited those around her. She even apologized to Mariela, didn't apologize exactly, but politely produced stacks of journal articles exploring tango from a feminist, from a Marxist, from an LGBTQ angle, acknowledging that she had deeply misunderstood the complexity and history of the dance and *oh, by the way*, did Mariela know the real history of the word "tango"? *Let me tell you...* Her enthusiasm disarmed even Mariela, whose defensiveness melted into wary interest in Helen's discoveries. Helen had a talent for this, it was why she was the kind of professor who attracted groupies: she carried with her a joy of learning new things. Towards the end of class she was exchanging *gazpacho* recipes with Andrew and promising Kev to watch a short film he'd made with his friends and posted online. Rosalind looked around for Bobby. She'd forgotten about him in the muddle of the past week and realized she hadn't seen him all night.

"Last dance," she heard him say.

"Oh! I didn't see you," Rosalind said, flustered, as though he could see she'd been thinking about him.

"Good to see you. Rosalind?"

She nodded.

"Bobby?" she asked, pretending to strain for his name in her memory.

"Yeah," he smiled.

"I didn't see you before," she said.

"Yeah, got here late. My girlfriend blew it off again," he said with a sigh.

"Really? I can't get my husband to come," she said. As usual, the steps came easily with Bobby. She didn't even really have to think.

87

"What are we gonna do with these people, Rosalind?"

She laughed. "I know."

She turned, struggling to keep her feet near the ground as she performed the *ocho* in front of him, as Mariela had instructed, not hiking up from the knee but keeping the raised foot just hovering over the floor, the sole subtly turned out, creating a "prettier line."

"I can't imagine a boy that doesn't want to dance with you."

Rosalind laughed nervously and tilted her head down in case she was blushing.

"I know, crazy, right?"

When she got home she found Cal at the computer. Writing.

"Wow." Rosalind said, pleased.

"Yeah. Been on kind of a jag. Where were you?"

Rosalind gave him a look.

"How'd it go?" he asked sheepishly.

This was more than they'd spoken all week. Rosalind flopped on the armchair wedged into the office's corner.

"Good. Mom's made everyone her adoring audience so now she likes it."

"You like it?"

She shrugged.

"Mean it's not full of handsome Latin men trying to seduce you?" he asked.

Rosalind smiled, pleased that Cal could imagine *anyone* trying to seduce her. She tossed her hands in the air, dismissing the idea coquettishly.

"You ever going to come to a class?" she asked pointedly.

Cal shifted uncomfortably in his seat, rising to find himself a beer in the fridge.

"Doubt it," he said, standing in the doorway.

"Why not?"

"Not my thing, I guess."

"What's your thing?"

Cal smiled, at a loss. She looked at him, the edges of his former self emerging. She missed that former self.

"Let me show you the steps," she suggested.

"That's OK," he said, waving her off, resuming his seat at the computer.

"C'mon —" she grabbed his hands rolling him in his office chair into the kitchen. He smiled as she pulled him out of his chair and put his right arm around her back.

"It's easy, you step, let's see... you step left then forward, forward, and then I do this thing — hang on."

They both laughed though an uneasy tension hung between them — a moment that could vanish as quickly as it appeared. She showed him the eight-step which he followed haltingly.

"See? You're a natural."

She raced to the computer, downloading tango music before Cal's mood suddenly changed. Cal made a face, indicating how ridiculous this all was, but raised his arms around her nevertheless. His movements were uneven; he was a natural athlete but maybe not an instinctive dancer.

"I think if you keep your feet lower, like let them glide instead of raising them? That's it," she told him.

The song started over again and Cal moved to turn it off but she stopped him.

"Just one more?"

It seemed to please him to give her something simple, something he could easily give.

"What kind of guys are at this class?" he asked finally. Rosalind shrugged as though she was unimpressed with the whole lot of them.

"Marrieds and gays, mostly," she said.

"So no gorgeous Latin lovers?" he asked.

"You're kinda hung up on the hot, Latin guys you think are sexing me up."

"Are they?"

They both fell silent, moving with greater and greater proficiency to the music and they noted, both without a word, that they had gone from doing steps to dancing.

"There's one guy I dance with who's straight," she said; it suddenly seemed dishonest not to mention him.

"Aha!" Cal said playfully, the accusing lover. "Found out."

Rosalind smiled. "He has a girlfriend."

"How good looking is he?"

Rosalind hesitated.

"Pretty good looking."

The song started up again but Cal didn't move to turn it off. They did the steps but this time he pressed his body against hers, holding her tightly. In class this was called "close embrace." In their kitchen it was called foreplay and she could feel his warm, beer-scented breath sweeping across her ears and nose, his lips finding hers. He kissed her forcefully. He moved to her neck, moving down her breasts and finally lifting her skirt and pulling her underwear slowly over her hips and down her thighs. Rosalind stood against the kitchen counter, hands braced against the sink. She was right, she was absolutely right. Buenos Aires was the answer to everything. Just a few clumsy tangos across the kitchen floor and sex was back. They had to move, tomorrow if possible. He would write, she would paint, then they'd dance and laugh and make love. It didn't have to be a fantasy. Happiness shouldn't be a luxury, she thought, as Cal's tongue found, lord help her, she couldn't think of it as anything else, her flower. They needed this, needed sun and dance and freedom. Were their passports in order? She wriggled out of the underwear bunched around her ankles. She bent over the kitchen table, lifting her skirt as he entered from behind.

"This OK?" he asked, moving in and out. He meant was the position comfortable, he was always considerate that way. Rosalind nodded, noting that at eye level the saltshaker needed refilling. No matter. They wouldn't need salt where they were going. She could already feel herself start to come in waves. They were definitely going to Argentina.

ten

HOURS LATER, ROSALIND AND Cal were still a naked heap on the kitchen floor. Somehow they had managed to fall asleep there as well, probably wouldn't have even woken till the morning had it not been for the incessant banging on a door nearby. These neighbors! Most of them were fine but there were the odd clutches of families with lone prodigals who showed up at all hours roaring motorcycle engines, shouting drunkenly. And then there was the house rented by a slew of new college graduates that had an endless stream of friends drifting in and out, playing dance music and making a big loud show of how young and carefree they all were.

The banging continued, louder and more insistent.

"Rosalind — the fuck are you?"

Oh hell. It was *her* door and *her* prodigal. Rosalind pulled on her skirt and shirt quickly, a hasty survey of the kitchen unearthed no underwear. She raced to the door, unlocking it and shushing a loud, hysterical Polly.

"Come in, what's happened?"

Polly moved past her, wiping tears from her reddened cheeks.

"I need a drink," she said walking to the kitchen and then stopping in the doorway, taking in Cal's bare ass and the bra hanging off the stove.

"For people who never do it you sure do it a lot."

"Polly. What's going on?"

Cal finally responded to the bright lights, the full kitchen. He blinked and stared at Polly, confused, as though he thought he might still be dreaming. Polly stepped over him, going for the liquor cabinet.

"Why don't you have some water?" Rosalind suggested.

Cal rose to his knees, grabbing a nearby pair of pants to hold to his crotch.

"Puhhlease," Polly said, "Do you have anything besides gin? How do you people not have vodka?"

Rosalind, realizing she wasn't going to be able to sell her on the water idea, produced a beer from the fridge. Polly looked at the label and made a face.

"They oppose their workers unionizing," she said.

"You want the beer or not?"

She did, taking a place on the couch, her elbows resting on her knees. Cal took the opportunity to walk into the bedroom and fall face first into the bed, fast asleep.

"What's happened?" Rosalind asked, taking a seat next to Polly.

"Mom and Dad threw me out," she said, staring at the bottle, picking at the label of her beer.

"Why?"

Polly shrugged.

"Polly…"

"They're totally overreacting."

"To what?"

"It's totally stupid. Totally unfair," Polly said, her temper rising as she replayed the events in her mind. "I can't believe the whole stupid system. I mean, it's totally corrupt and people are just supposed to be these indifferent robots buying deodorant and cars and cloned food and vegetables full of toxins and if anybody opposes it they just get crushed. Fucking crushed!"

"Polly, calm down. Just tell me what happened."

Polly took a large swig from her bottle, wiping her nose with the back of her hand.

"I mean, you know who *should* be in jail right now? The fucking CEOs of Monsanto. I mean, how many people have they destroyed? How many people have they killed? But nobody cares cause they've got their TVs and their *happy meals* and—"

"Polly. I can't talk to you when you're like this. You're going to have to calm down." Polly had her tirades but it was rare for her to get this emotional.

"Fucking *Monsanto…*" Polly sobbed.

Rosalind went to the kitchen to grab the glass of water and wet a clean dishtowel, pressing it against Polly's forehead, wiping away new tears.

"Take a deep breath." Polly did. "And tell me what's happened."

"I mean, nobody cares that honeybees just totally disappeared. It's like: *whatever.*"

"If you're gonna start in on the honeybees, I'm going to bed," Rosalind told her.

Polly nodded and took another drink.

"I need a cigarette," Polly said.

"Cal has some hidden in the garage. He thinks I think he quit."

Polly headed out the back door and found a pack of American Spirits without effort, taking a seat on the back steps. She lit one and took a deep drag, sighing out smoke. Rosalind followed her out, pulling up a moss-streaked plastic lawn chair and sitting.

Polly stared up at the night sky with narrow-eyed scrutiny, as though the story she was about to tell had been written there.

"So. Bryan," Polly began, "and his group are investigating companies that are manufacturing seeds and such — y'know all these strains they're inventing. Turns out there's this big lab here doing major research developing this strain of seed resistant to fungus and pests but they think it might have to do with the disappearance of honeybees. I mean, they don't even know what it does and what it kills, they just research and develop and sell the motherfucker and they buy off the sad-ass families that start having three headed babies. I mean, that's how they do business! It's all about quarterly profits and shareholders and—"

"Why did Mom and Dad throw you out?" Rosalind asked trying to keep Polly on track.

"This lab had a security camera which we totally didn't see."

"You broke into a lab!?"

Polly nodded.

"What'd you do?"

"Destroyed the plants. Someone's got to stand up to them," Polly said, stabbing the air with her cigarette. "The police were able to identify Bryan. He already has a record — did some time for vandalizing SUV's in California."

"Jesus, Polly!"

"It's not that big a deal. I mean, they should be arresting CEOs not Bryan who's only trying to do good things."

"He was arrested? Were you at the scene?"

Polly nodded proudly.

"This is why they threw you out?" Rosalind asked.

Polly nodded again. "Mom said she didn't raise a thug. What the hell? That's the problem with people from the sixties and seventies — they think they invented social protest but they totally screwed up by selling out. I mean, just look at the world! *Good job, guys.*"

"Polly. You can't just go around breaking the law."

"You are so like Mom and Dad it's fucking pathet-ic," Polly cried, stubbing out her cigarette.

"What about the police, Polly? Did you ever think about that? This is serious."

"Only Bryan knows my name and he wouldn't give me up. He's not like that."

Rosalind rolled her eyes.

"He isn't!" Polly protested.

Rosalind felt overwhelmed with a desire to throttle her. Polly had inherited their mother's passionate opinions, but none of her charm, and the result was toxic. While their mother had the strange ability to win over even those who intensely disagreed with her, Polly had the reverse talent; she alienated the people who agreed with her. There wasn't a belief Polly held that Rosalind didn't share; she too believed that agribusiness was systematically destroying the environment and she hated the drug companies and oil companies and the cozy relationship between corporate America and the government; she worried — sometimes intensely enough to impress the likes of Polly — about the honeybees and colony collapse disorder and dolphins and the women of the Congo and religious intolerance and melting polar ice-caps, but there wasn't an instance in which she discussed these things with Polly in which she didn't come away thinking: well, it can't be *that* bad. Polly lacked the ability to moderate her thoughts, to temper or tailor them to her listener's hearing so that it all sounded like the deranged conspiratorial rambling of a sidewalk drunk.

"Well." Rosalind said calmly. "You can stay here tonight. We can figure things out in the morning."

"Thanks," Polly sighed before heading to the re-frigerator in search of another beer.

Rosalind opened the linen closet. She thought of being nice, of finding the air mattress and inflating it for her sister, until she saw her passively watching from the doorway, drinking her beer as Rosalind struggled with the blankets perched on a high shelf. Screw it, Rosalind thought. She's only here for one night.

eleven

IT WASN'T UNTIL MID-day that Rosalind got a phone call from her mother. The call came while she was in the middle of helping two customers and really couldn't talk. Bryan had indeed given the police Polly's name and her address and her cell phone number, he might even have given them her astrological sign for all Helen knew. Polly was being charged with breaking and entering and vandalism. Helen and Richard had already lined up a lawyer.

"The lawyer thinks they may let her off since it's her first offense, but they may go after Bryan for terrorism. Terrorism! Can you believe this? Like he's Bin Laden or something," Helen told her over the phone.

"Do you have this in yellow for infants?" a woman asked; she wore a baby carrier holding an infant so tiny it looked like a loaf of bread strapped to her chest.

"I think so. I'll be right there."

"This is what we pay taxes for?" Helen raged.

"Polly isn't a kid. She's thirty," Rosalind reminded her. In addition to all of Polly's crimes, she'd also derailed Rosalind's only memorable night with Cal in recent history; federal prison seemed like a fitting penalty. Still, Rosalind felt a quiet, buzzing happiness:

she and Cal had finally had a night they needed. They were back on track. Everything would be OK. Her instincts were right after all: Argentina, tango. She just needed to convince Cal. But how could he argue with last night? The woman with the bread loaf baby gave her a look of impatient longing.

"I'll have to call you back," Rosalind said, hanging up and approaching the woman. "Thanks for your patience."

She searched for a yellow sweater, telling her other customer, "I'll be right with you." He was a man in his thirties with a shaved head, wearing a trendy black retro polo sweater. He waved away her concern.

"I'm fine," he told her, smiling pleasantly at the clothes before stopping in front of one of the hummingbird paintings. She rang up the sweater and the woman left. The man was still scrutinizing her paintings.

"Who paints these?" He seemed to be glaring at her work.

"Me," she admitted reluctantly.

"Well, now. I had no idea I was in the presence of real talent."

She felt a rush of warmth spread over her. All for a stranger's approval, how ridiculous, she thought.

"You're very kind."

"It's not kindness. These are terrific. I really like," he said with a kind of smooth obsequiousness. He seemed as though he should have a cocktail in hand or as though he'd just wandered in while emceeing an awards show.

"I see price-tags. That means these're for sale?"

"It does. Hummingbirds were believed by Native Americans to be magical emissaries from the afterlife. Some people like to keep these in the nursery as

representative of someone who's no longer around —
like a grandparent. As sort of a benevolent spirit."

The man nodded, seemingly unmoved by this information.

"Is there a particular color you're looking for?
Sometimes the yellow or green is good if you don't
know boy or girl yet."

"Oh, god no. I'm not decorating a nursery," he
said and then laughed as though this was the funniest
thing he'd every heard. "God. No. I own the wine bar
that's opening up down the block, *Terroir*. I've just been
popping in to meet the neighbors and say 'hello'
so…hello!"

He held out his hand triumphantly like a returning
astronaut, "Julian Daniels."

"Rosalind Plumley," she said, taking his manicured
hand in hers, "Welcome to the neighborhood."

"Thank you much," he said, bowing his head.
Rosalind couldn't quite decide if his affectations were
charming or annoying. Possibly both.

"I wonder… Do you do custom jobs?"

"Of what?"

"Painting."

"I've done a few nurseries."

"I love what you're doing here," he said, pointing
vaguely at the painting. It had been so long since
Rosalind had been *doing* anything with her painting that
she didn't quite follow. "Aggressively pretty. It's almost
over-the-top but restrained. I'd love to get one of these
for the bar."

"Of course," Rosalind agreed, surprised.

"It's like the wallpaper of an Edwardian mistress. It
makes me think Wallace Simpson, you know? Only
without the Nazi sympathizing, of course."

Rosalind nodded as though this had been her exact intent.

"This'll be my second bar in town," he told her, apparently fearful that she might not realize what rarefied company she was keeping. "I also own *The Chess Club*."

"Oh."

"You've heard of it?"

She had indeed. It had been the subject of one of Glen's late-night rants about the mixology movement and the trendy bars popping up all over the city. He'd railed against their speakeasy pretensions and their grave, young suspender-clad bartenders obsessed with egg whites and bitters and cocktails that took so long to prepare Glen could easily polish off at least five Pabst Blue Ribbons before a Perfect Manhattan reached his table.

"Heard of it, never been. I hear good things though," she said.

Julian gave a patient nod, of course she had.

"The new one's all wines. Sustainable. It's all about sustainability. Lot of biodynamic. You know what that is?"

Rosalind shook her head.

"You will," he said, smiling confidently. "Please stop by next week as my guest, Rosalind Plumley. And I will be buying this painting. Brilliant!" She pulled the painting down off the wall and set it on the counter for him to admire more closely. "Yeah. This is exactly the look we're going with, kind of a funky nouveau Edwardian vibe, you know?"

Rosalind nodded: of course, of course.

"What's this music?" he asked. Rosalind sometimes put on tango music and practiced her steps behind the counter when the store was empty.

"Astor Piazzola," she told him.

He whipped out his iPhone, began searching, "How do you spell that? I want to play this at my bar."

"P-i-a —"

"Found it," he said and bought it in one click. "Perfect."

Her phone rang and she made an apologetic gesture before answering it.

"So they've set bail," Helen began.

"Hang on, Mom."

"Ah, Mother," Julian said and held up a hand to say she need explain no further.

"Sorry," she said. "It's just my sister's in jail." A revelation she immediately regretted. "I mean, not for like *murder* or anything —"

Julian gave a worldly, dismissive wave of his hand as though sisters and jail always went together. "I'll pick this up later," he told her in a stage whisper. She smiled and nodded gratefully, returning to her call.

By the time Rosalind returned home, bail was posted and a sentencing date set. She found Cal on the couch watching *Kill Bill, Volume 2.*

"Didn't you just watch this?"

"I wasn't really watching."

Cal paused the movie, running his hand through his hair and then rubbing his eyes.

"So. I'm not sure how much of any of this was a dream, so you tell me: we had a lot of sex and then Polly was yelling about stuff and then she was arrested."

"That all happened."

"Anything else?"

"The lawyer says she needs to get a job to prove she's a viable member of society."

"Huh," he said, un-pausing the film, "You've been saying that for years."

They watched again for a while, Rosalind waiting for Cal to say something about their night together. Wasn't he also thrilled? Hadn't they turned a corner? She had been mentally planning to reintroduce the Argentina plan, had been rehearsing the words that might sway him. Last night seemed like a good place to begin.

"Speaking of a lot of sex—"

Cal looked at her quizzically as though he didn't know they were having a conversation. Was he supposed to pause the movie? Again? He gave a slight sigh to indicate what a concession this would be and within that fleeting gesture Rosalind lost her nerve, in fact, felt again the crushing embarrassment of trying to fix anything with something so grand, so life changing, so non-pharmaceutical or practical as an extended stay in South America.

"It was nice," she said.

Cal nodded.

"I sold a painting."

"Good for you."

"Yeah, this wine bar owner bought it. Said I was brilliant,"

"You are," he said affectionately before returning his gaze to the television. They watched like that for another half hour; Cal indifferent and Rosalind in a kind of sinking desperation only amplified by television: all that color and spectacle over something that didn't matter at all to her. By the end of the movie she was in a familiar stupor and looking forward to sleep when a knock at the door announced Polly's release from jail.

"Hey," Polly greeted them, flopping on a chair in an exhausted heap. She didn't mention the fact that she was, yet again, their uninvited guest, in fact, acted as though she, not they, were performing a great favor, and regarded Rosalind with an ironic, patronizing smile when asked why she hadn't gone home.

"I can't. Not until I get a job. I mean…" she sighed loudly, "I wouldn't *need* to live at home if I *had* a job," she explained in the circular logic that defined her entire adult life.

"She has to go," Cal said in bed that night.

"I know."

"Please don't do that thing you do," he said, a request that required no elaboration. Rosalind's role as a pushover in her family was well established. She was the peacemaker, the defender of one faction against the other, the tireless advocate of the irritating and the unreasonable. She felt the middle child's eternal obligation to hold the center and it occurred to her at times like these that it was a thankless job, one that possibly didn't even need doing. She indulged when, as Cal often insisted, she should take a stand. Rosalind knew he was right but still felt the sting of an attack. He was, after all, criticizing a tendency toward indulgence that he himself exploited, one that over the past few months had possibly been the only thing keeping their marriage intact. But, as she listened to Polly crash around in their kitchen, wordlessly judging their food choices and liquor cabinet, she knew he was right. Polly had to go.

twelve

Rosalind and Cal barely spoke anymore and they both found reasons to be gone from their home, a place that had been taken over by the invasive creep of Glen and Polly. On the first night Rosalind returned home from work during Polly's stay she found her relaxing on the sofa in Cal's usual spot and Glen seated in his chair, an empty pizza box between them.

"Sorry we didn't save any for you," Polly told her unapologetically.

"I thought you were vegan," Rosalind said, wondering what errand she could invent to get herself out of the house.

Polly shrugged. "Vegan pizza just totally sucks."

"How's the job search?" she asked.

"Some leads," Polly told her vaguely.

Glen nodded, packing a new bowl. Rosalind had already warned Polly off Glen ("don't sleep with him, don't mention Radiohead"). She knew they'd get along. They both shared the ability to stretch one subject — their superiority to all others — into many hours covering, among other things: which seasons of the Simpsons were brilliant and which were crap; why American movies were no good anymore (ditto, music), why Portland was over-run with hipsters even though no one ever self-identified as one and how, in fact, Portlanders (they excused themselves from this company) were driven by fads but smugly believed themselves above them; why Scorsese, Shakespeare, Thomas Pynchon, Bob Dylan, and Virginia Woolf were all wildly over-rated; why liberals who patted themselves on the back for watching *The Wire* were pathetic and how the corporations were taking over and privacy no longer existed and nobody cared as long as their iPhones worked.

Rosalind had always had Glen pegged as one of what she called authenticity hunters: tribes of urban discoverers in search of the best, the truest place to live. They arrived at each new destination only to pronounce it dead; full of hipsters and posers and yuppies. According to Glen, who was a refugee from a depressed logging town in Washington State, Portland was already over. He was always planning an escape but never making it. He had speculated on a back-to-basics life on one of the islands outside of Seattle but then met a man in a bar with the same idea and abandoned it.

Hour after interminable hour, Rosalind overheard Polly and Glen's discourse while trying unsuccessfully to read a book in the other room, plotting their murders before deciding to attend her first *practica*.

The *practicas* were supposed to be just that: practice. They were open sessions for anyone at any level to drop in and hone their skills. Rumors of the *practicas* had filtered back to the beginning class from a few enterprising students who'd given them a try and like soldiers returning from the front, circulated tales of strange and frightening things. First off, the *practica* was really no place for beginners. If you lacked skills you stood on the sidelines feeling like the worthless reject that you were. And it was no fun. Everyone took themselves too seriously, don't waste your time until you've been dancing the tango for a while.

Rosalind had heard all the stories and been properly chastened by them, but driving home from *little fig*, contemplating another night of Glen and Polly, she followed an impulse and drove to the studio instead. She liked to think she was at least an above average dancer in her class, comments from Barry and Mariela suggested as much. She was learning more advanced steps like the *barrida* and the *molinete* and the *sacada*, names that sounded to her like jet-set prostitutes. She walked into the dance studio which had dimmed its lights to give a nightclub feel. The reports had been true: these people took their dance very seriously. Grim looking men and women locked in a grave ritual moved at varying rhythms around the floor; they displayed fewer of the ornate maneuvers Rosalind would have expected of advanced dancers and supposed that the embellishments associated with ballroom tango were out of fashion here. The dance was largely one of attitude, with an air of serious, contemplative movement. Rosalind took her place on the sidelines, observant and self-conscious.

She was relieved to see another person from her class, Tracy, a young customer service representative who was cheerfully tormented by her singleness. "All my friends are married! Kids. The whole boat," she'd told Rosalind during class break once, "I'm like the last of the Mohicans!" Rosalind and Tracy stood along the wall, smiling pleasantly as though watching were the sole purpose of their visit. Rosalind watched one couple. The man, tall, with bushy salt-and-pepper hair and a mismatched suit, danced with an equally tall, dark-haired woman with an expression so severe she seemed to be angry at tango. Their dancing was simple and expert and reminded her of something one of her art teachers told her about bad artists taking something simple and making it seem complicated while good artists took something very complex and made it seem simple. The couple was an illustration of this rule; the dance seemed to barely qualify for the term — in essence they seemed merely to be walking, slowly, in lockstep. They would stop occasionally, the woman led into a simple *ocho* and then resume their slow, meditative procession. They seemed, to Rosalind's untrained eye, to be under a spell.

A Russian man in his fifties, smelling of after-shave and chewing gum asked her to dance. She had noticed many Russians amongst the unexpected pockets of ethnicity represented in her class (thirtyish Asian men being another). The man seemed to go in for complicated steps that Rosalind didn't yet know or couldn't remember so that their dance felt more a like a series of syncopated apologies and miscalculations. Rosalind had thought herself a reasonably promising beginner but as it turned out she was an absolute disaster and the men she danced with that night were all too ready to tell her exactly how. The Russian man told her (after first asking if she'd like some tips, something she'd learned was part of the tango etiquette; one never offered advice unsolicited but once permission was granted the floodgates opened and the judgment flowed) that she was too tense in her right wrist and that she needed to put less pressure against his left hand.

The next man told her that her wrist was too *relaxed* and she should apply more pressure. It went on like this all night. She raised her foot too much (something she was already aware of), she anticipated the man's lead, she was tense. Strangely, she didn't experience what other beginning students had at the *practica* who said they'd been totally neglected; she had a quick succession of dance requests accompanied by lectures both solicited and unsolicited detailing her many faults. Each partner got three songs broken up by an incongruously raucous polka, during which men asked the women (and, of course, it was always the man asking) for the next dance.

One partner finally gave her the most helpful bit of practical advice: "Look at the man's top shirt button," he told her. "His torso will tell you where he's going."

Rosalind nodded though this new knowledge proved untrue; she still had no idea where a man wanted her to go, top button or no. This was something she had asked about in class and never received a satisfactory answer: how on earth could a woman tell where her partner was directing her? Mariela had only told the ladies that they should simply stop moving if the man's lead was unclear, a bit of advice that would have brought the beginning class to a crashing halt. "Ladies, don't fake it," she'd told them with a smirk, "it's true in tango like everything else. If you fake it, the man never learns!" Everyone would give this a matching little chortle. Barry would raise his eyebrows amongst the men to indicate his lady *never* had to fake it. And then the ladies went back to faking it, if only to get to the end of the class.

She decided to take a break and went in search of the drinking fountain. She walked down the long hallway paved in pink linoleum marbled with brown swirls making the building feel like the relic from the fifties it probably was.

"You're not leaving?" asked the man in the mismatched suit, the one she'd been watching earlier.

"No, I —"

He took her hand and led her back to the studio as the polka music ended. The tango began and the man didn't move, simply swayed, inviting Rosalind to do the same. She anticipated moving sideways, even moved her right foot to the side, alone.

"Relax," he told her, an instruction that, as usual, caused her entire body to go rigid with tension. She tried desperately to relax. She focused on her breathing; she tried not to think about the next step, she tried to ignore his halitosis (the bowl of hard candy at the studio's entrance suddenly made sense). She was, she knew, stuck in the beginner's paradox: in order to perform well the steps have to become second nature, happen without thought, but Rosalind was nowhere near that stage and therefore had to think.

"Who are you taking classes from?" he asked.

Rosalind gestured towards Barry and Mariela.

The man inhaled sharply. "You're not learning real tango."

"Really?" That was news to her.

"You shouldn't learn steps. You move. Intuitively. Slow down. We don't have to get anywhere. It's like making love. It's better when it's slow."

Rosalind laughed nervously. "OK. Good to know!"

How did one reply? Any chance at relaxing was gone. Who said these kinds of things? To strangers! Rosalind wished her mother had come just to hear the speech he'd get if he spoke to her this way. She laughed again, trying to cover her intense desire to flee. Why had she come anyway? Sitting on the couch and listening to Glen gas on about fixed gear bicycles now seemed like a thing of joy next to the constant criticisms and unsolicited dance/sex advice. This dance was stupid and these people with their stern looks and serious shoes exhausted her. Now she knew why that lady looked angry at the tango. It was hateful.

"Relax."

Rosalind curbed an impulse to walk out and never come back. She did stop swaying.

"I'm sorry but tense is the way I am tonight. You're just gonna have to deal with it," she told him, her voice heavy with exasperation, with the strain of holding in all the things she'd like to say to him, to Cal, to Polly, to the whole damned mess of things.

The man smiled, pleased. "OK," he said.

It occurred to her that following didn't mean passively accepting whatever was thrown her way. She could push back. They walked and walked. No fancy steps. No *ochoes* or *barridas*, just slow, stealthy progression around the line of dance. He'd stopped pointing out her faults and she'd stopped caring. So what if her wrist was rigid as a highway divider? The thoughts of all her obligations — her hours on Craigslist looking for a job for Polly or researching alternative therapies for Cal's depression (his meds clearly weren't doing any good), or untried fertility aids (raspberry bark tea, cranio-sacral massage, acupuncture, tincture of chasteberry and on and on...) — suspended momentarily; they hadn't disappeared, only hovered. But she was, at least for two more songs, mercilessly released from their crushing burden. She didn't have to do anything or go anywhere but move slowly back and back and back again. There was a sweet nothingness to the walking tango. She hadn't forgotten herself, instead, she felt absorbed. Absorbing states. She'd read somewhere they were healthy, these times during which the minutes passed without realizing it. It was a creative state. The most creative state. She used to have them. When? In college. Before college. She used to paint and paint for hours and not care what the hours amounted to or how much she could sell it for on the walls of *little fig*.

She shouldn't have gone to New York. That ruined it. Then it became about competition and knowing the right people and "presenting well" in class. She'd had one year of art school in the city before calling it quits, returning as — what felt to her — a failure. Her father had been consoling, he'd hated New York too; people cared about the "wrong shit" there. But it still felt like a personal failing. It wasn't for lack of will, she arrived feeling full of promise but wilted in the presence of so many interesting, glamorous personalities. She couldn't keep up and didn't really care to. By the end of her first week she was so intensely homesick she would phone home in tears. How embarrassing. People should be able to leave home; it was a sign of weakness, she'd told herself, that she couldn't tough it out.

And then she met Cal. They went to a movie, a Peter Weir retrospective showing *Picnic At Hanging Rock* (possibly the worst first date movie they'd both agreed later) and then had a drink during which Rosalind confessed her shame at leaving art school, at being so old and still suffering from homesickness, and Cal convinced her there was no shame in loving home. No shame at all.

The next song was plaintive and simple, a woman's desperate grieving set to music. The lyrics were basic, the singer's love had wilted just like a flower, but something about the singer's pain hit Rosalind. She had been pregnant a few months when she'd had a dream in which she asked people what her child would be like. Every time she asked, her vision would fill with cherry blossoms — only that — the breeze moving through pale pink, nearly white, petals. Person after person, each time she asked the answer would be an image of cherry blossoms. What did it mean? Even in her dream she was perplexed.

When she woke up she looked it up online. Cherry blossoms represented a short but noble life; the Japanese revered them for their brief lifespan. Kamikazes were known to paint them on the sides of their planes. According to Buddhist thought, cherry blossoms represented the transience and brevity of life. Brevity of life as in the normal span of a human or something much shorter? She got her answer later that week when she and Cal went to her second ultrasound and she looked at the screen anticipating the sweet pulsing heartbeat she'd seen at the first.

"I'm very sorry," the obstetrician said.

"Oh, Plum," Cal said, squeezing her hand.

Her doctor told her "it wasn't meant to be" and that they could try again but after all, he said, lifting his palms to the heavens with an exasperated sigh, this is what happens when women wait to have babies. The receptionist, unaware of what had happened, congratulated them as they left.

"I'm so sorry, Plum," Cal said as he drove her home. She was in tears, he was numbly stoic. He was patient with grief. He knew it well. He didn't tell her to get over it or that they'd just try again. He knew not to offer false comfort, unlike others who greeted the news with: "At least it happened early." Some days the sadness seemed to travel through her like a shard of glass she'd swallowed, slowly and stealthily slicing through her insides. Cal didn't require her to get better quickly. He'd let her weep in restaurants and quietly paid the bill. He understood.

"You're doing better," her partner commented as the song ended.

"I wasn't really thinking about it," Rosalind admitted, roused from her thoughts.

"That often helps," he said, bowing deeply from the waist.

Rosalind had barely noticed the song pass in and out of time. The crazy polka began again. Rosalind thanked him for the dance as well, said her goodbyes to Tracy, and then Barry and Mariela, and headed home. She had hated most of the *practica* except the last heady six minutes, but with a junkie's conviction decided to return again for more.

thirteen

A FEW WEEKS INTO THE class session, Helen and her coterie of gay boyfriends launched something of a velvet revolution. Helen, citing her continuing investigation into the gender roles as defined by tango, expressed an interest in learning to lead.

"There aren't enough men as it is anyway," she added on a practical note.

Mariela and Barry looked a bit dumbfounded by the request — as teachers they had both learned to lead and follow, but students rarely asked to cross gender lines. But ultimately they were performers at heart and believed in giving people what they wanted.

"I'd actually like to learn to follow too," said Andrew, a dark haired, bookish looking man in his twenties, though he may have rethought this after being crashed around the dance floor a few times by Kev. He and Kev had begun a quiet romance. Rosalind had learned this from Helen who kept close tabs on these things.

"Men and men. Totally," Kev agreed. "Just like on the Pampas," he added, his inflection making the Pampas sound like the hottest nightclub this side of the Andes.

After that class a handful of students learned to lead *and* follow. There was a clubby joyousness to the class that hadn't existed before. Even the most stalwartly masculine of the (usually) older men were at least bemused by the developments, even as they insisted on dancing with women.

"I love watching these old guys' eyes when I ask them to dance," Kev whooped with laughter after a second margarita. This had become an after-class ritual over the weeks; margaritas at a Mexican restaurant called Mimi's just a couple blocks from the studio. It was really a ritual of Helen and the gay boyfriends and whoever else showed up. Sometimes it was just Helen and Kev and Andrew and Rosalind. Other times, Felicia and Bethany, both women in their twenties, showed up; Felicia with blond ringlets and Bethany, a pierced nose, who had taken the class with Kev and Andrew. Sometimes Paul, the retired architectural engineer joined them. Even Barry and Mariela had made an appearance. It was a place for Helen to hold forth on what she was learning about her new obsessions: the gender politics of tango, the history of tango, Argentina and its troubled, fascinating past.

She reviewed Argentina's colonial history, the evolution of the Pampas as an economic driver. She talked about Peron and the Dirty War and the Falklands.

"Did you know the word 'Argentina' means land of silver? Its very name locates it as a source of riches, a place driven by economics."

She covered the 1989 economic collapse (a result of the costs of the Dirty War and then The Falklands); how it resulted in 10% inflation per month; how the treasury disastrously tried to solve the problem by simply printing more money, and how that plan reached its end when the *treasury literally ran out of paper* to print the money on; how the economy recovered slightly in the 90's only to crash again in 2001, sparking an ongoing crisis that romantic-minded Americans and Europe-Europeans could now take advantage of through the still beneficial exchange rate; how the history of Argentina was one of shocking economic bungling and cruel, torturous political games that left its landscape and people battered and continuously exploited from the appearance of its first Spanish sailor.

Her audience would nod appreciatively and order another pitcher. It was during these interstitial moments, between her mother's set speeches and rants, that Rosalind would learn the most. She was used to seeing her mother amongst her adoring charges and protégés, but these students were different, irreverent, bawdy.

"Helen, how long before you're screwing Paul?" Kev asked one night when Paul was absent. Paul was a pleasantly bland widower in his sixties who wore V-neck sweaters on even the warmest nights. He looked too much the cheerful golfer for Rosalind to ever picture him with her mother.

"Oh, stop. That crap is over in my life," Helen told him. There was something about the gay boyfriends, their directness disarmed her, she revealed more than Rosalind had learned in a lifetime, it felt, in these few short hours over watermelon margaritas. One night Helen was commiserating with Andrew, who had recently split from a longtime, live-in lover.

"It's the worst feeling," she said, staring off vaguely, lost in another decade, "it's really the most shattering moment when you stop being enchanting to someone else. You're suddenly… just this person. And so is he." Her audience nodded thoughtfully. Rosalind, watching from the corner of the table, her head resting against the wall felt something like a quick rush of air, as though she were falling suddenly, unexpectedly, through space.

"Are you talking about Richard?" Kev asked.

"Of course! Who else? But that was ages ago," she said, quickly regaining her mirthful pose. "And yet twenty years later you're learning to tango and drinking margaritas. So to hell with it!"

"To hell with it!" they all agreed, raising their glasses. But all Rosalind could think of was twenty years. Twenty years of feeling unloved. She had, for all of her mother's frank sex talk, never actually thought of Helen as a sexual person, that is, someone who desires and is desired. Or someone who desires and isn't desired back and is heartbroken by it. She wanted to ask her mother but didn't dare. Kev and Andrew could ask her things she never could, casually, over drinks. Her mother had allowed herself to be an enigma to her daughters all the while pretending to be the hippest, most open, most tell-me-anything kind of mom. What little she knew or understood of her parents' strange arrangement consisted of this: at too young an age (Rosalind tried to recall, she was seven, maybe?) her parents sat the girls down and described an infidelity on Helen's part which, in their mania for openness, they described with both physical and emotional candor the Plumley girls would spend the entirety of their lives attempting to forget. Her mother had never apologized for the affair and her father had therefore never forgiven her.

But, as Rosalind reordered the past in light of this last revelation, if her father stopped loving her mother, maybe she felt justified. Maybe it was her right. Rosalind had always blamed her mother for the split, perceived it as part of her fetish for being interesting. Her father had previously seemed blameless in the matter, the victim even, of Helen's voracious ego. Now the pieces reordered themselves. Rosalind watched her mother whoop with laughter as she ordered another round. Rosalind imagined a woman with three children whose husband has stopped loving her. She fears she will never be loved and the fear makes her silent. The silence finds voice in an affair. She feels justified for her betrayal since, in her mind, it comes in response to his much larger sin: he has ceased to find her enchanting.

How had it escaped her, Rosalind wondered. How had she never appreciated that her mother was a human being with her own desires and disappointments?

"I think I'm finally ready to do it," Helen told her audience. "I'm buying dance shoes."

Kev applauded. Bethany begged to go with her.

"*Beware all enterprises that require new clothes*," Andrew said archly, draining his drink.

"*And not rather a new wearer of clothes*. People forget that part," Helen cheerfully reminded. "Thoreau. That old cluck. Y'know his mother was washing his clothes while he was staring out at Walden Pond? I swear, every time a man has some epiphany, dollars to donuts there's some woman nearby doing his wash."

"I'll go with you," Rosalind offered. Helen fixed her with a look of real surprise.

"I didn't think you'd be interested."

"Of course I am. I've been going to the *practicas*. I'd like to go shopping with you."

Helen nodded and her eyes even seemed to mist up a bit — though this often happened after the second margarita.

"All right then," Helen agreed.

fourteen

DANCE SHOES, LIKE MOST things in life, seemed to favor women with high arches and narrow feet. There were shoes of the Bond girl variety on the far left wall, shiny champagne colored strappy heels and vertiginous black patent leathers with peekaboo toe-holes and femme fatale ankle straps. Helen and Rosalind both had flat wide feet that severely limited their choices. Fortunately they both preferred the utilitarian offerings featured on the "basic" wall. The store had three walls of shoes that appeared to progress from right to left in order of insanity. The shoes on the right wall included the simple black shoe with a low heel and a lone strap that Rosalind recalled were also referred to as "character shoes," worn by the bossy young women in high school who reliably always played the lead in every school play, and would show up to the first day of rehearsal as Ado Annie or Betty Rizzo in a pair. Helen bought these. Rosalind chose a slightly more embellished version: it had a narrower, higher heel and was held in place by two black straps that crisscrossed at the top of her foot.

"Tell me what's happening with Cal," Helen commanded over lunch at a Thai restaurant, a quiet place in a converted house along a busy street with white tablecloths, pink orchids in vases, and a young waiter who bowed so heavily at the neck he seemed to be apologizing for taking your order.

"He's fine. Busy. DimeEdge is rolling out a new campaign and they're adding a line of kids' clothes, so yeah. He's busy."

"And how're you two?"

Rosalind hesitated and considered using the moment to ask her mother about what she'd said to Kev the other night. Instead she smiled nervously, unfolding and refolding the paper sleeve of her chopsticks.

"We're good. It's just… Polly." She gave a shared look of exasperation. "She just sits around all day online and sighs a lot."

"She tell you about the settlement?"

"Settlement?"

"The lab settled out of court. For her, anyway. They realized she's not anyone of particular clout in that group. They're going after Bryan and his friends. But she has to pay restitution."

"She never said anything," Rosalind said as her pad Thai was set in front of her.

"She wouldn't. She has to pay five grand in restitution."

"Jesus."

"I know," Helen nodded. "Turns out that lab's pretty evil. They'll probably end up killing us all," she said, piercing a baby corn with her fork. "Read some of the articles Polly gave me. Have you? They're truly horrific."

"And she has to pay them? How's she gonna make that kind of money?"

"Especially without a job," Helen shook her head.

"Honestly, Mom. You guys have to take her back. We can't do it anymore."

Helen sighed. "I know." She stared down at her food and then out the window, gazing at the passing cars pensively. "I'll talk to Richard. You've done more than you should. We know that." Helen started eating again and then casually asked, "How are you?"

"I'm OK," Rosalind assured her.

It felt strange having a mother-daughter talk. Rosalind couldn't remember if that was something they ever actually did. She usually guarded her personal life from Helen.

"Well. Take care of yourself," her mother told her with what seemed like planned *gravitas*.

Rosalind nodded. "I will."

Rosalind's cell phone rang. She looked at the phone's display: a number she didn't recognize and a name she barely remembered, Eric Ames. She instinctively picked it up.

"Hello?"

"Is this Rosalind Plumley?"

"Yes."

"Your husband's here. You should come over. He's fine but… well, you should just come over."

"What's happened?"

"I think he might be high or something. I mean, he comes over a lot to walk Jordy and all but —"

"He does what?"

"Oh. I figured you knew."

Eric Ames lived in a dark wine-red single story house at the end of a block of blue and gray and white houses. Rosalind climbed the two steps to the door and knocked.

"Hi," he said, letting her in.

The interior was painted in various shades of grays and greens and yellows — tasteful, trendy colors; if Rosalind had seen the rooms photographed in a magazine she would've torn out the pages, stuffed them in a file of design ideas for the future and then never looked at them again.

"Nice place," she said.

"Thanks. Actually credit goes to my wife, my ex-wife. She was a designer. Well, she still is," he told her. "Cal's out back." He led her through the kitchen to a small backyard tastefully landscaped with indigenous plants and bushes. Cal was asleep on a wooden chaise.

"Passed out a little while ago," he told her.

The dog slept next to him, waking suddenly with their arrival. Rosalind was struck by the ordinariness of the dog. In the context of Eric's home, he was free of the threat she'd felt before. He was, she realized, just a dog. They both watched the slumbering Cal.

"What happened?" Rosalind asked.

"He was fine when he came over. Went for a walk with Jordy and came back a couple hours later, I was just in here grading papers and he was obviously pretty out of it. Then he started apologizing — to me, to Jordy. And then he fell asleep."

Rosalind went to him, considered waking him.

"Oh," she sighed. "He's been kind of depressed lately," she explained to Eric. Eric nodded as though this confirmed his own theories. He looked at her, raising his hands in a "now what?" gesture and they both smiled, flummoxed by the moment. There was something about the way he moved — his long, slender fingers extended gracefully like a dancer's — that was strangely soothing to her.

"Would you like some cake?" Eric asked inexplicably.

"Sure."

He led her back into the kitchen where he produced a white box from the refrigerator. "It was my birthday yesterday," he told her. "How big a piece do you want?"

"Happy birthday. Just a little — that's fine."

"Some of the teachers chipped in and got me this. Had a little party."

"That's nice."

"Yeah. Should I make some coffee?" He set down her plate in a breakfast nook painted in a kind of gold iridescence.

"Don't go to any trouble. We've already bugged you enough today."

Eric shook his head, he seemed eager for the company. "How about dessert wine? Do you like dessert wine? I have this stuff from France that's supposed to be really good but I never really entertain so it just sits there."

"Um. OK."

Rosalind sat down, noticing the walls in the nook and the dining room and living room were all bare with only the occasional empty hook indicating a previous life. She noticed the faint, square outlines, ghosts of disappeared wall hangings.

"My ex took all the prints," he explained.

"Oh."

Eric grimaced, indicating it was no great loss. "They kinda creeped me out actually. There were these black and whites photos of flowers that just looked...I don't know...angry. Angry flowers. I was kinda glad to see them go."

Rosalind nodded. "This cake is really good," she told him.

"Oh! The dessert wine," he said remembering and then withdrawing a long, thin bottle from an upper cabinet. He took out two small glasses and set one down in front of her, pouring her a glass.

"You know much about wine?" he asked.

"Hardly anything. I keep meaning to. It's seems like it's required all of sudden."

"It does, doesn't it?" he said, as if genuinely struck by the thought. "When did that happen?"

Rosalind shook her head.

"Janine, that's my ex, she'd order a sixty dollar bottle of wine in a restaurant and to tell you the truth, I couldn't tell the difference from just some cheap, old bottle."

"Maybe it's cheaper not to know the difference."

"Yeah," he said laughing. "That's for sure."

They fell into silence eating cake and sipping the sweet dessert wine. He finally held up the glass of wine to the light, observing the amber color.

"Think this is any good?" he asked importantly.

"I have no idea," Rosalind admitted. "Tastes good to me."

"Me too," he agreed.

Rosalind pushed a piece of frosting around her plate, preparing to ask the questions she was clearly required to ask.

"Sorry about Cal. How long has he been coming around?"

"Ever since Jordy came back. It's been a big help actually. I leave early in the morning and I'm sometimes not back till seven, eight o'clock. Having someone to walk him has been great. Jordy's stopped trying to get out. It's been great actually." Rosalind nodded, realizing

Cal hadn't been going in early to work and hadn't been staying late as he'd told her. Lying was becoming a thing with him.

"You probably think it's weird he never told me," she said. Eric shook his head as though he'd heard weirder things. "I notice you call the dog Jordy now too."

"Yeah. It's really a better name for him. I hated calling him Prince. It was Janine's idea."

"How long have you been divorced?"

"About a year. Separated longer."

Rosalind raised an eyebrow.

"Why?" he asked.

"I would've guessed you split more recently."

"Really? How come?"

"You mention her a lot."

"Do I?" Eric smiled sheepishly and studied the outlines of picture frames on the wall. "You ever read *The Alchemist*?" he asked. Rosalind shook her head. "Janine went on this trip with a girlfriend to Mexico and read *The Alchemist* and then came home and said she wanted a divorce. Just like that. Said if I wanted to understand why she was leaving it was all in there."

"Was it?"

"I haven't brought myself to read it. That's not true. I started it and it just seemed kinda pretentious. I don't know. She said she'd always thought it was fate we were together but when she read that book she realized nothing's fate; it's all choices and she'd made the wrong ones. We both had."

She nodded sympathetically. She sensed Eric Ames didn't have a lot of people to talk to.

"I don't know. Maybe she was right," he said. "She was really into brunch. You know those people that'll stand outside for hours just waiting to get into the new, cool place every Sunday? She was like that."

"I love brunch too," she told him guiltily.

"She also cheated on me."

"I'm sorry."

He held up his arms in a pose of cosmic befuddlement. "Hey," he said philosophically, "like the guy says: it's all choices."

They both laughed wearily.

"I guess so." Rosalind studied the walls again, her gaze wandering the kitchen and then startling at the sight of Cal, framed in the doorway.

"What are you doing here?" he asked Rosalind.

"We should go," she told Eric.

"How'd you get here?" Cal asked her, still in a fog.

"C'mon. I'll drive you home," she told him. "We'll pick up his car tomorrow, if that's alright?"

"Sure. Thanks for coming by," Eric said sincerely, if somewhat nonsensically.

"Thank you. And happy birthday," she said, as they eased Cal into the front seat of her car, his shoulders stooped as though his body didn't quite believe it was awake.

They barely spoke on the way home. Cal dozed and Rosalind couldn't find the words to ask what was happening. When they arrived back at their house he insisted he was hungry, sat down on the couch with a jar of peanut butter and promptly fell asleep again. Sleep and silence had become the latest means of shutting her out. Rosalind pulled his feet up on the couch, telling Polly nothing more than they'd both had a long day and then took a long hot bath and thought about what she should do about Cal. What was there left to do to help? What hadn't she thought of yet?

The next morning she waited until he was awake and asked, "What are we going to do?"

"About what?"

"You. The dog. What's going on?"

He rubbed his eyes and massaged the small of his back. He'd slept the whole night on the couch.

"I just like the dog. What's the big deal?" he asked.

"What did you mean about him being Jordy?"

Cal winced. "I know it sounds crazy but he just… it's like his spirit, animus, y'know, whatever it's called. You just look at me like I'm crazy —"

"No, I don't!"

"Yes, you do. You look at me like I'm crazy all the time."

"So, you think he's like your brother reincarnated or something…?" Rosalind asked, straining to sound as non-judgmental as possible

"No. Sort of. You don't know what it's like."

"Well, then *tell* me what it's like, stop walling yourself off," Rosalind pleaded.

Cal nodded, she had a point. He searched the air. "It's like nothing will ever feel good again. Ever."

"Maybe we could try the Lexapro instead —"

"It's not something you can just take a pill for," he said.

"What does Gene say?" Gene was his therapist.

Cal held up his hand angrily. "I know you're trying to help but just stop it. Stop trying to fix everything like it can be fixed. I don't want Lexapro and I don't want to go to Argentina. I just want to spend time with a dog and smoke a little weed sometimes. OK?!"

"OK," she said softly.

He walked out the front door, slamming it behind him.

Mood swings, Rosalind told herself, but she felt stung just the same and her stomach rumbled in agitation. Then she remembered they still had a car to pick up.

Rosalind took a cab over to Eric's house with one of her hummingbird paintings under her arm. She had brought it as an apology of sorts, but as she stood waiting on his doorstep she had time to question her plan. Why had she brought a painting? It was too much. He would think she was weird. Even worse, he would *know* she was weird. Or that she was coming on to him. Was she coming on to him? She'd been married so long she hadn't even thought about it but, oh no, worse still, he would think she was conceited! He would think she went around giving out these paintings because she thought that they were good. Which they were not. She was a delusional sad lady painter trying to seduce nice men with her sad lady paintings. That's what he'll think. Did she have time to get the painting back to the car?

"Hello! This is a nice surprise," he said.

"Happy birthday," she told him, offering up the painting, "I thought you should have something for your walls," she explained as though she were merely solving a design problem.

"Hah!" he said with a delighted laugh, taking it from her hands and immediately stalking his house for the best place to hang it. "It would be more prominent in the living room or dining room but this is where I actually spend a lot of time these days," he said, placing it on one of the hooks on a wall in the breakfast nook. "You don't mind?"

"Why would I mind?" She was pleased he was pleased.

"You're very thoughtful," he said, admiring it. "Fact, you're the only person who gave me a gift this year."

"I am?" she asked. Now she was glad she'd brought it.

"No biggie. I'm thirty-five. That's the age the Buddha achieved enlightenment."

"Good to see you've set yourself realistic goals."

Eric smiled.

"It's also sort of an apology for yesterday," she explained.

Eric shook his head, confused.

"I mean the trouble we've caused. Cal," she explained.

"You haven't caused any trouble. And you don't need to apologize for Cal. If anything, sounds like he owes you an apology."

Rosalind smiled, agreeing to this felt like an admission of something larger and so she remained silent.

"I should go," she said finally.

"No. Stay. I've made coffee." He poured her a cup, not waiting for her answer. They took seats on the patio in matching dark wood chairs with green and blue cushions, no doubt the work of the stylish and absent Janine. Rosalind sighed deeply and listened to the wind in a maple tree whose branches stretched from a neighbor's backyard to canopy half of Eric's. They smiled at each other awkwardly.

"I wanted to ask you something," he said, setting his cup down emphatically.

"OK."

"Who is Jordy? Cal sort of references someone else but he's never really made it clear who the other Jordy is."

She set down her cup and looked at him squarely.

"Cal's younger brother. He died in a hiking accident when they were teenagers. Cal's always blamed himself."

Eric nodded soberly.

"He thinks his brother's the dog. Or his spirit is in the dog. Or something," she explained.

"Maybe his brother *is* a dog."

"Who knows?" she said, throwing up her hands.

"My grandmother had a smoke alarm that would beep occasionally and she was convinced it was my grandfather saying hello from the afterlife. I mean, she knew it was nutty but she didn't care. It made her feel better."

"Sounds like the battery needed changing."

Eric laughed gently. "I changed it. It still did it."

"Maybe she was right then."

"There's all kinds of ways of looking at things."

"Yeah, I guess so," she said, looking up to see the wind blowing through the high branches.

"Sounds difficult."

"It is, but he is trying. He's seeing a therapist and he's… I don't know, he's trying."

"No, I meant you. It must be very difficult on you."

Rosalind looked down at her lap and nodded, she felt her shoulders quake with emotion, with all the energy it took to muddle through. She shielded her face from him.

"I'm sorry. I didn't mean to upset you," he told her.

Rosalind shook her head, embarrassed. Maybe Cal was right and nothing would ever feel good ever again. Eric put a hand against her cheek and she felt how cool it was, how nice and cool against the raging hot of her brain. She held it there like a wet compress, feeling ridiculous and soothed at the same time. *I should go, I must go*, she told herself.

"I'm fine," she finally managed. "I should go," she said, standing hastily, the sudden movement sending her emotions back under control. She reached the front door without even realizing she'd fully formed the intention to leave. She opened it.

"Hey," he said, reaching her. He held his arms open and she let him hug her. They stood there a long time, Rosalind lost track of how long. She felt his coffee scented breath against her neck. His shirt smelled of dryer sheets. She imagined he was compulsive about clean laundry. She sensed something she hadn't since her single days, the moment when attraction tipped over into inevitability: This is going to happen. And then another certainty: I better go home. She pulled away abruptly.

"Thanks. It was good to see you," she said absurdly and headed for Cal's car.

part two

Everything changes. Nothing is lost.
- Ovid

fifteen

INSOLENT. IT WAS A good old word but virtually never used anymore except when employers were firing Polly. In the hazy unreality that was the last few weeks of the summer, Polly had been hired and fired twice. Both jobs had been promising, one at a used bookstore, the other at a gluten-free bakery. And she was still sleeping on an air mattress in Rosalind and Cal's office.

Rosalind's emotions were steadily trickling out, getting the best of her. She hadn't been sleeping, she had no appetite, she found herself getting irritated by small annoyances, snapping at Polly. She and Cal had negotiated a weary truce of sorts, an arrangement that felt to Rosalind more insidious than outright conflict.

"You're probably wondering why you married me," he said casually over coffee one morning.

"No, I don't," she'd protested.

"I would if I were you," he said.

Rosalind stared at him, astonished and he stared back. She thought he might cry.

"Cal —" She took his hand in hers. He pulled his hand away and abruptly left for work.

At *little fig* that morning an irate customer stormed into the store demanding a refund for a handmade receiving blanket. Rosalind had hoped for a quiet day but had already had a rush of yoga mommies in and out of the store and now this.

"It shrank!" said a woman with tight-fitting jeans and tousled, expensively blown-out hair. She looked like a rich California transplant, the type Rosalind didn't particularly care for but often found herself defending to Polly. She was clearly a new parent, a first-time new parent, the class of people so tyrannized by the demands of a screaming, non-sleeping infant that whenever possible they exacted the same demands on those serving them. New parents were typically the most difficult customers and any parent shopping at a store like *little fig* already had a fair sense of entitlement, to say nothing of their children, suffering as they did from what she and Cal had dubbed PBS, or Privileged Baby Syndrome.

"The care instructions say it has to be hand-washed," Rosalind explained. She turned the item over several times trying to remember when they'd stocked it before realizing:

"This isn't ours. We've never sold these."

"I don't know where it's from," she said, heaving a sigh of exasperation. "It was a shower gift!"

"I'm afraid I can't return this then."

"You're joking. What are you going to do for me?" she demanded, holding up the offending item, a now tiny blanket made from a patchwork of vintage Japanese silk fabric that was possibly the most foolish thing ever made for a baby. She did make an excellent point: you really *should* be able to throw anything for a baby in a washing machine.

"It's not our store policy to return items we don't sell," Rosalind tried to explain rationally.

In moments such as these with difficult customers Rosalind would sometimes try a technique she'd learned in a meditation class: imagine your mind is the sky and troubles are like a cloud floating past. She tried it. She even took a deep, cleansing breath. *My mind is the sky, my problems are just clouds.* But staring across the counter at the woman with her $1200 Coach handbag and $5000 nose and the Lincoln Navigator parked illegally outside, all Rosalind could see was the injustice of wealth.

Oh, how much better could Rosalind spend that money! She would be in Buenos Aires right now and Cal would be finishing up his day of writing because things were going so well and he wasn't depressed anymore and didn't believe his brother was reincarnated as a brown Labrador and they would make love because that was something that happened often between them again and then they would wander down to a late dinner with their new friends, Kurt and Freya from Germany, and they would all drink red wine and laugh and then that odd but charming British guy, Geoff, would show up and bum cigarettes off Kurt even though he was rumored to be worth twenty million dollars from something to do with computers and then someone — Rosalind or Freya, usually — would suggest going to a *milonga* to dance and there would be a plume of dissent, *oh no, we went last night and danced till three in the morning, we're not in our twenties, we can't do it again*, and then Geoff would order more wine and then suddenly there'd be a second wind and they'd all be out dancing again until three in the morning and swear that *tomorrow, tomorrow, they would finally stay in for a night at last.*

"What are you going to do for me?" the woman asked again.

"This is from another store. I can't refund your money," Rosalind said.

"I don't think you are *hearing* me," the woman said in an emphatic, patronizing tone. She heaved her important, tanned breasts against the counter. "I want a full refund. *And* an apology."

"You do understand that not all children's stores are the same store?"

"I don't have time to run all over town finding out where it's from!"

Rosalind sighed deeply. "Can't you just ask the person who gave it to you?" The woman reeled back as if she'd been slapped across the face.

"That would be rude!"

"I'm sorry but I'm afraid I can't help you."

"I'd like to speak to the manager."

"She's out of town." Ingrid was, at that moment, sunning herself on the island of Corfu. "I can have her call you when she returns."

The woman huffed mightily, untangling her big sunglasses from her hair and putting them on. "I will be speaking to your manager."

"I'll let her know," Rosalind said but the woman was already out the door, replaced with unnerving gravity by the strange wine bar owner from down the street. He walked to the counter and smiled gravely.

"I'm thinking of sexy grapes," he said.

There was a charge about him as if he had just embarked on a magnificent journey and if you were very lucky he would tell you about it. She didn't have the energy for him.

"Julian," he said, reintroducing himself.

"I remember."

"Big, sexy, libidinous grapes," Julian continued, standing in front of her. "I want you to paint them. Over the bar."

"Really?"

Rosalind flipped the "back in 15 minutes" sign that she used for coffee breaks on the door and followed Julian down the block to *Terroir*, the name of which he had recently had stenciled to the outside of the building and Rosalind consistently misread as "Terror."

"You haven't been in yet," Julian noted with a joking flirtatiousness.

"Sorry, yeah. It's just been—"

"That's OK. Here we are," he said, unlocking the door and ushering her in. The bar had been painted in deep shades of brown and had low built-in booths in a square modular design. Bars always seemed a sad thing in daylight to Rosalind and this one in particular felt exposed by the harsh glare of daylight leeching through the glass front.

"It's nice. How's business been?" she asked, looking around.

"Only been open a couple of weeks but it's getting known. Had a lot of people over the weekend so we're getting word of mouth. Keep losing waitresses though. Jaaaysus, that part's hard," he said.

Rosalind smiled sympathetically.

"That's where I want your sexy grapes," he said pointing to an expanse of wall over the long curved bar. "What do you think?"

"You want something that fills the space?"

"That's right. Only thing, I can't pay you upfront, my money's all tied up right now."

Rosalind nodded, she knew bar and restaurant owners to be a shifty lot, always complaining about investors, going broke, suddenly leaving town.

"So if we could do some kind of deferred thing? And you could leave your cards out, if you want. I've already had people asking me about that one," he said, gesturing to her hummingbird painting over a booth in the corner.

"Uh…well," she said wavering until an idea occurred to her, "You're looking for wait staff?"

"Eternally," he sighed.

"My sister's looking for a job."

"She have any waiting experience?"

"Yeah," she lied. Well, it wasn't a lie exactly; Polly had lasted half a day at the gluten-free bakery.

Julian smiled. "Send her my way."

"Shipping a wine all the way from France? Oh, very fucking sustainable," Polly griped, tossing aside the wine menu Rosalind had brought from *Terroir* to show her. She'd phoned Polly from work about the job offer and then her parents, convening an emergency Polly's-moving-out council at her parent's home that evening. Rosalind had played up the devotion to sustainable winemaking she thought would appeal to Polly and played down Julian's desire to create a "funky nouveau Edwardian vibe" which she knew would not. The four of them sat gathered around the dining room table.

"Rosalind's gone to a lot of effort to help you find this job," Helen told her. "I think the words you're looking for are *thank you*."

"Just doesn't make any sense, is all," Polly explained. "He's all about the environment but shipping stuff from Italy and France? Hello? Local wines, much?"

"He has local wines. A lot," Rosalind protested.

"Still. Shipping this other stuff across the ocean and then trucking it across the country. Yeah, no footprint there," Polly snorted derisively.

Helen threw up her hands, exasperated. She was a mystery to her sometimes, this humorless daughter.

"They're mostly local wines," Rosalind assured her, rubbing her eyes, "there aren't a lot of biodynamics in America but they're a growing trend. He has a proven track record. He owns *The Chess Club*."

"Do they actually play chess there?"

"No, I think he just likes the name."

Polly rolled her eyes. "Barf."

"You will not be this ungrateful girl," Helen told Polly, slapping the table for emphasis, "you will not be my daughter and be so ungrateful to Rosalind. To me and your father."

Polly raised her eyes and then looked down again, examining her fingernails.

"I think what Helen's saying," Richard said after a long, tense silence, "is you're really not in a position to negotiate. Take the damned job. Move back into your old room." It was the rare occasion in which anyone needed to clarify what Helen was trying to say. Rosalind looked to her mother to see if she minded. She didn't. He looked around for confirmation. "Everyone OK with that?"

Rosalind nodded, satisfied. Polly nodded. Richard rose from the table and made his way back to his studio. Polly stayed with their parents that night. Rosalind went home alone. Cal was probably back to his dog-walking routine. In any case, he wasn't around and as usual hadn't communicated when he'd be home. She opened a cheap bottle of red wine, opening the windows and letting the cross breeze cool the house, which was stifling in the late August sun. She went into the office where she put Polly's things in neat piles by the door to be picked up in the next few days. She dismantled the air mattress, deriving near opiate pleasure from the whooshing sound of air exhaling from its cavity. It was the sound of the last guest leaving. Rosalind finished her glass of wine and, ignoring her hunger, climbed into bed and fell asleep.

sixteen

IT WAS ALWAYS *SOMETHING* WHEN Eric Ames's name appeared on Rosalind's cell-phone. She was still at *little fig* but picked up anyway.

"I don't want to alarm you."

"What's happened now?" she asked, dread already knotting her stomach.

"I got this check. From Cal. Do you know anything about it?"

"A check? For how much?"

"Five thousand. For Jordy's surgery."

"Hang on," she told him, her heartbeat already racing.

She went online and checked their bank balance. Nearly half of their joint savings had been transferred to their checking account. There was a long pause on the telephone, which Eric finally broke.

"I had a feeling he didn't tell you. I'll just tear it up."

"Don't — I want to see it," she told him.

"What?"

"I want to see the check."

It was a Saturday afternoon. Ingrid would be back from vacation the next day. Rosalind closed the shop early, even though Ingrid liked her to keep it open later on weekend nights to catch the foot traffic of people coming and going from bars and restaurants. But she couldn't stay in the shop another minute. She had to see the check.

She went to Eric Ames's red house at the end of his block. She walked up the two stairs to his door and knocked and listened as his footsteps grew closer and the door finally opened. She felt an awareness that she should feel embarrassed under the circumstances, without actually feeling so. She felt electric, like she was going to catch on fire.

"It's in here," he said, matching her urgency, leading her to the now familiar breakfast nook as though she were a paramedic showing up to the scene of an emergency. A bluish-gray rectangle of paper with Cal's handwriting sat on the table. Definitely his handwriting, Rosalind confirmed though there had never been any doubt. She wasn't sure why this fixation on seeing it herself. She held it in her hand. She sat down and stared at it, a sick pain in her gut. She felt the rickety supports holding up her marriage come clattering down.

"Do you want some water?" he asked.

Rosalind shook her head. "I'm fine."

"Do you need a paper bag?"

"Why would I need a paper bag?"

"You look like you're hyperventilating. A little."

"No. No, I should go —" she said, standing.

"You're upset," he said, guiding her back down. "Give yourself a minute."

They sat wordlessly, only the sound of an oscillating fan breaking the silence.

"It's really not even necessary," Eric said, gesturing to the check. "I've been saving up for the surgery myself."

Rosalind nodded.

"Actually some people advise against ACL surgery in dogs. It's somewhat controversial. Anyway, I was going to do something about it myself," he said a little defensively. "Just all my money's sunk into this house. Bought out Janine and you know, teacher's salary and all."

Rosalind only made out a few words of what he'd said. She kept looking at the check, folding and unfolding it. Cal had done a lot of things but she'd never thought him capable of this. She knew he wasn't well, wasn't rational but still... he should have it in him not to be cruel.

"How did you end up teaching?" she asked, the sound of his words was soothing even if she only made out a few of them. If she could listen long enough maybe she could pull herself together and get as far as the door and then where? Where could she go?

"Came to it kind of late. I had another career. A ballet dancer, actually."

"Really? Professional?"

"Uh huh. I know. People never expect that. Ballet dancer to algebra teacher — kind of not a typical career path. But it's the usual story: I injured my knee — ACL as it happens. It's funny, you spend your whole life as a dancer knowing you're just one injury away from it all being gone — you're always afraid of it — and then one day it happens and it was kind of a relief, weirdly enough. It finally happened. But I was still, as you can imagine, pretty desperate so I started thinking what else I liked, what I was good at. And I always loved math."

Rosalind watched him gesture with his long, narrow fingers, suddenly aware of a desire to put one in her mouth.

"How long did it take you? To make the switch?" she asked.

Eric shrugged. "A week maybe?"

Rosalind nodded absently. She felt an urge to lie down on Eric Ames's slate grey kitchen tiles and hold him next to her. It wasn't sexual, she told herself. She just wanted the calming presence of a kind stranger. She should go, she should really go before she did something she couldn't undo. She put the check in her purse, suddenly ashamed. How embarrassing to travel all this way to have a stranger witness your worst, most humiliating moment, to see you emotionally stripped, unloved and unwanted. She rose unsteadily, stabilizing herself with the table.

"Whoa, hang on," he said, rising with her and grasping her by the shoulders. "Sit just a little longer," he pleaded. He filled a glass of water and made her drink.

"I'm really alright," she said, sitting back down.

"I know. Just indulge me," he said, smiling.

Rosalind cracked a smile. "How long were you married?"

"Almost three years. You?"

"Married for six but we've been together over ten."

"Long time."

Rosalind nodded wearily. "Keeps getting longer."

They both laughed sadly and she rose again to her feet.

"Really. I'm OK," she assured him. "Thanks for calling and letting me know," she said, trying to wrap things up.

She studied his long fingers with their black smudge marks and imagined them travelling down her body. She looked up at him and kissed him. She felt hesitation on his part, an obligatory, moral one; she was a vulnerable woman just dealt an emotional blow. He should be levelheaded and noble. She felt this impulse

146

and then felt it dissolve as his hands pulled her closer. They kissed with a kind of hurried frenzy as though they knew one of them might regain sense and stop things. Neither of them did. Eric lifted her t-shirt over her head and fingered the clasp of her bra.

"Wait," she said, stepping back. She looked at him, the high, pale cheekbones flushing red. Charming, dutiful Eric, the former ballet dancer. He'd had his dreams dashed and yet he recovered the same week. Who made quick recoveries like that? How could he be trusted? She felt for the clasp of her bra and unsnapped it.

She walked towards him, taking one of his narrow fingers in her mouth and then leading it down to her breast. They made love like lonely people, at turns grateful and awkward and hungry. Thoughts of morality filtered in and out of her consciousness but they felt beyond her; she couldn't think past what she needed to feel better, right now. The future, the past were merely hazy abstractions. She felt an odd sense of relief — like the dancer who spends life fearing the one final injury — she'd been flirting with infidelity since that first tango class without even fully realizing it. Straying had been the constant threat. Here it was and it felt good.

They stayed in bed for a long time afterwards. It was dark and they said nothing; both of them too awkward with one another to voice anything like regret or pleasure. Rosalind had entered a new club she'd never thought she'd join. She'd cheated on her husband. It had happened. But she felt guilty in only the most conceptual way. Infidelity, adulteress, betrayal; hard Old Testament words that might show up on her deathbed and usher her to eternal suffering (how was it — and what did it mean? — that she, essentially an atheist with no real belief in God or heaven, could easily entertain notions of a hell?). Hadn't Cal's check represented a greater rupture? Hadn't he rather passively (he didn't even have the decency to own up to it!) already left her?

Eric Ames paid attention to her. She was the object of scrutiny, affection, desire. Lust. It didn't matter. Those slender fingers and hungry kisses. She wanted black smudge marks all over her.

She finally broke the silence, staring up at the ceiling of his bedroom.

"I had a miscarriage. Almost a year ago."

"I'm sorry." Eric stroked her arm.

"And then like a month later we were driving to the coast for our anniversary and really for me to feel better since I'd been depressed and we were headed out of the city and there was this pigeon who'd been hit by a car but wasn't dead, it was flailing. All over. We were going through this underpass and it kept rising and falling and flapping its wings wildly and getting hit again, rising and falling and getting hit. I lost it. I couldn't stop crying and I couldn't tell Cal why I was crying. It seemed silly but also like the worst thing that had ever happened in the world. You're a bird flying along and then WHACK you're struggling for your life and bloody and getting hit, not once but over and over. There was nothing I could do for it. It just kept flapping away, like it knew it was doomed too but it wasn't done yet. I never told anyone that story. I don't know why I'm telling you."

He ran a long finger over her forehead and smiled.

"What?" she asked, embarrassed. She'd revealed too much. He was surely wishing she'd leave.

"You're sad, Rosalind. It's OK. I am too."

He wrapped her in his arms and they fell asleep. When she woke the next morning she was disoriented to find a tastefully stark room, not the piles of books and clutter that littered her and Cal's bedroom. The room felt curated by an art director for Pottery Barn instead of lived in by a human. Eric woke just as she was noticing the matching apothecary lamps on the nightstands.

"Did you sleep alright?" he asked.

"I did. You?"

He nodded and they kissed and then parted without a plan; they didn't agree to see each other nor did they swear never to do it again. They parted like two people in a trance.

seventeen

ALONG THE UPPER BERTHS OF the Broadway Bridge a great chorus of birds sang loudly from the canopy of steel under a darkening blue sky. It was one of Rosalind's favorite sounds but their chatter was frightening that morning, shrill and deafening as she drove home. A strange impulse caused her to stop at the saddest flower store in the world. Mr. Hoffman's store was dusky and dark and, unusually, inhabited by two other customers. They looked like they had wandered in by mistake.

"Haven't seen you in a while," he said to Rosalind, more of an accusation than greeting. He rose reluctantly from his seat at the register where he usually sat staring at his empty store. Rosalind wandered the aisles simply inhaling its wilting green melancholy. She heard Mr. Hoffman harrumph approvingly when she picked a handful of irises and some bachelor buttons.

"Thanks," one of the two departing customers said as they both ducked back onto the sidewalk.

He waved goodbye to them and then returned, with a strange enthusiasm, to the flowers Rosalind was trying to buy.

"You are nice to buy him flowers," he said in a brief spasm of pleasantness. Rosalind smiled, unsure why she'd felt compelled to buy sad flowers. They weren't for Cal. Not exactly. They were to mark the occasion. Things had changed and would continue to change. She and Cal had been miserable for months, with themselves and each other and now that was going to change at last. They would trade their current miseries for new ones.

"Haven't seen your husband in a while."

"He's been busy," she told him.

He tipped his head to the side as though it were no matter to him. He finished wrapping the flowers in faded polka-dotted paper and took Rosalind's money. As usual, he charged too much.

"Thanks," she said and hurried out of the store, flowers under her arm. She walked slowly to their house, unsure what she would find there and what she planned to do. She wanted to be honest. That was as much of a plan as she could manage: be perfectly honest. She saw Cal's car was in the driveway. So was Glen's bike. She heard doleful Russian music fill the house as she entered and found Cal and Glen watching a movie.

"Hey," Cal said, not lifting his eyes from the screen.

"Hey."

"Hi, Ros," Glen said.

Rosalind watched them. They were watching a documentary on Stalin.

"Cal?" Rosalind asked finally.

Glen rose to his feet, smelling tension in the air. For a stoner he was pretty sensitive sometimes, Rosalind noted. He slipped on a pair of flip-flops and made his way to the door.

"Call you tomorrow, man," he said, leaving.

Cal turned to Rosalind, unsure why his wife was staring at him with a bouquet of wilting flowers. "What?" he asked.

Rosalind sat down next to him.

"When we were driving to the coast for our anniversary and I started crying and I couldn't tell you why. There was this pigeon that got hit on the freeway and it kept trying to fly up and then it would get hit again. That's why I was crying. I wanted you to know that."

Cal looked at her quizzically. "OK. I just figured it was the miscarriage. You were pretty emotional."

"Well, yeah, I guess that too."

Cal took her hand, stroking it gently. Rosalind felt a surge of panic and guilt. Why was Cal so cruel as to write that check and now so kind? It wasn't fair.

"And I slept with Eric. I wanted you to know that too."

Cal's hand went still.

"Who?"

"Eric Ames."

"The guy with the dog?"

Rosalind nodded, staring ahead at the flowers she'd bought, still encased in their fading paper wrapping. Cal shook his head sharply.

"I don't understand. *The guy with the dog?*" he asked again.

"He called about the check. For Jordy." Cal just kept staring at her with that quizzical look.

"I didn't mean for it to happen," Rosalind heard herself say. She felt the strange sensation of her life falling away from her.

"When?" he asked.

"Last night."

A long silence passed between them, electric with the energy of two people debating what to say next. She

eighteen

ROSALIND AWOKE UNDER A MOBILE she'd made in college. She'd been in her Calder phase, somewhere between Velazquez and Kiki Smith. She made it out of Lucite pieces that caught the morning light as it came into her girlhood bedroom. Nothing had changed since the day she'd moved out at eighteen. In the confusion of waking she forgot she had grown up and moved out. *Someday your marriage will fall apart. You'll live at home. You'll be in your thirties. Late thirties. You'll cheat on your husband. Cheater. You'll feel emotionally justified but still feel like shit. Possibly forever.*

She stared up at the motionless mobile dangling over her bed. Five uninterrupted days of *little fig* lay ahead of her, five days of onesies and diaper bags and tales of Ingrid's Greek vacation and the impatient demands of new parents. She turned over in bed and listened to squirrels chase each other across the eaves of the house with an astonishing, loud rattle.

It was a graveyard of sorts, her room. She kept all her artistic phases here: the high school paintings from her Matisse phase and college shadow boxes inspired by Rauschenberg, filled with news clippings, vintage postcards, sad old doll heads, mousetraps, and fishing lures. She'd never liked them; they were just grubby and menacing junk struggling to mean something, an odd combination of murder scene and the floor of her parents' basement. She admired her friends who were able to produce such things without it seeming like a pose; they seemed to dash off works that smelled of glue and formaldehyde and foundation grants while she labored mightily, trying to create raw and challenging work. It was kind of a relief to finally produce what she naturally gravitated towards, unfashionable representational painting, label it ironic and be considered, at the very least, clever.

She longed to fall back asleep but her memories were only waking her up. She was dimly aware that she should make up some kind of story before going downstairs; she sometimes stayed at her parents' home if she was visiting a friend nearby or if Cal was out of town, but she usually didn't sneak in during the night.

A slight draft moved the mobile pieces in slow drifting circles. She remembered an undergraduate fascination with chance, with the flexible orbit of mobiles and how they changed with time, the environment and the light. She'd liked the idea of randomness being contained within the artwork itself, available to future actions, to something as simple as a light breeze on an August morning. The red and pink and coral pieces of plastic were shaped like shells and birds; Rosalind had begun to play with prettiness, with "received notions of femininity" — or something like that. That's what she remembered, or at least what she told the fashionable friends she wanted to impress at the time. Her work had developed quotation marks around it, lest anyone think she took it seriously. Looking up at the mobile now she took a pure pleasure in its beauty. Maybe she had never been ironically commenting on beauty. Maybe she just liked it.

She pulled herself out of bed. She could hear movement downstairs. Coffee and toast and newspaper headlines that were already producing effusions of disgust. She threw water on her face and pulled on some extra clothes stashed in her room, a pair of gray shorts and a faded denim shirt. Making her way downstairs she was still uncertain what excuse she would use for her sudden appearance until she saw her sister frowning at the contents of a cereal box and decided to use a strategy that had worked in virtually every situation since childhood: blame Polly.

"I decided to give Cal the house for a while. With Polly there so long it's been a pretty full house. Thought he could use a little time to himself to write," she explained to Helen, pouring herself some coffee and sinking into a chair with the newspaper.

"You know how much shit I'm having to memorize for this stupid job?" Polly asked her.

"Oh, good Lord, Polly. Let's not start that all over again," Helen said.

"I'm having to learn about California wines," she said, horrified. "*California* wines!"

"They are a major wine growing region," Rosalind remarked dryly, refusing to look up from the paper.

"California wines. In the *Pearl District?*"

Polly couldn't let it go, she could never let it go, the fact that Rosalind now worked in the Pearl, an area once only occupied by Powell's Books, the yeasty smells of the local brewery, warehouses and the untended railroad tracks where at least a couple teenage Plumley girls were known to drink beer amongst other underage friends. Today it was: Whole Foods, West Elm, Anthopologie, expensive condos, *little fig*, and now, *Terroir*.

"Stop being so tragic," Rosalind said, staring out the window where crows argued with one another in loud, squawking wails. She wondered if she should call Cal.

"Well, he can fuck off if he thinks I'm going to push anything other than local wines," Polly said.

"Polly, leave your sister alone. She's in a pensive mood," Helen told her as she took her coffee and disappeared into her book-lined study.

"I mean the whole concept of *terroir* is you're tasting the region, that it's part of the wine's nature. What's the point of tasting another region when you're here?" Polly complained, staring down at the tasting notes she was trying to commit to memory.

"I don't know. Maybe people want to know what other regions taste like," Rosalind said.

She took her coffee and wandered into her father's study, a small and dark room covered on every wall by art books. She pulled one down, Rilke's letters on Cezanne. She'd read it as a teenager and while it had a deep influence on her she probably hadn't read it in over a decade. She'd been thinking about Cezanne's still-lifes ever since Julian mentioned painting sexy grapes. She leafed through the book, looking for something vaguely remembered: *Surely all art is the result of one's having been in danger, of having gone through an experience all the way to the end, where no one can go any further.*

She returned to her bedroom, opening all the windows. The air was still now and the colors hung stationary, at attention. She lay down and stared at the mobile. She would occasionally raise her leg to give the objects a slight push with her foot sending them back into orbit. She watched them move and slow and move again, colors bouncing in space, reflecting the light. She thought about Julian's grapes and the meeting she was supposed to have with him that afternoon to discuss her ideas. Her mind drifted to Eric and the memory of his body pressed against hers. She didn't know what to make of how much pleasure his body brought hers. Guilt and self-justification took turns with her mind like that all morning as she watched the colors reflected on the wall grow larger and smaller. She drank her coffee and read from her book, finding a quote from Cezanne: *we live in a rainbow of chaos.*

She managed to keep her appointment with Julian to discuss sexy grapes and perhaps even start tracing their outline on the wall.

"We don't open till six, so anytime before then, you can work on it," he told her. "I know, I should've done this before we opened but I was kinda going with a sparer look but all I do is stare at that wall and think, God, we need some color in here, some life!"

"Something beautiful."

"Exactly," he agreed with a grateful smile.

"I'm thinking layers of color, especially reds and purples, so there's a deep, matted look to it — maybe highlights of silver giving a kind of iridescence that'll play with the light," she explained.

He nodded, staring at the blank wall gravely. "Yes, yes."

"You want something that isn't just decorative but expresses the idea of *Terroir*, this idea of place informing what it produces. The look of the grapes are going to change with the light in here, the move from day to night, going from natural light to candles."

Julian nodded and frowned as though he hated the idea but Rosalind learned this was his look when he intensely agreed.

"Yes, absolutely."

She set about a preliminary outline, based on sketches she'd shown him. She had assumed she'd be left alone to work but Julian used the advantage of his captive audience to share everything he knew about biodynamic wines. Rosalind was trying to simply concentrate on the task at hand, it was the only way to disconnect from the riot of emotion recalling Eric's slim wrists and slender fingers discovering her neck, her back, her thighs.

Rilke had said of Cezanne that the "good conscience" and "truthfulness" of his reds and blues could heal one of indecision once and for all. She looked up at the outline she'd soon fill with color and thought: *Please heal me.*

Julian's conversation wasn't boring but she couldn't have been less interested in learning about wine at that moment. He described his first trips to France and the odd winemaker he'd met who turned him on to biodynamic wine. Great armies of details marched *en masse* against her brain's indifference and she was compelled to absorb a phalanx of new facts.

"Sulfites are highly controversial!" he told her.

"Uh huh."

"Some vineyards are organic but forego the official designation because of all the hassles and paperwork involved — and by the way, organic and biodynamic are different. But sometimes they overlap."

"Right,"

She didn't want to be rude, but he was making it awfully hard to concentrate as she stretched to reach the upper portion of the wall.

"Biodynamic mostly has to do with the purity of the winemaking, it's about respect for the land and the vines and all of nature. This Austrian spiritual ethicist came up with it and it involves a bunch of crazy, mystical practices like burying a cow horn full of dung or yarrow flower fermented in deer's bladders or planting vines along specified astral lines. Now, I don't know about all that, but I do know their wines are generally superb."

"Yeah?"

He then went on to describe his own personal history, which involved moving up from San Francisco four years earlier to open *The Chess Club* with his investor, Ehren Ffolkes.

"You've probably heard of him," he said, polishing a wineglass with a white cloth. She shook her head. Julian repeated Ehren Ffolkes's name with such frequency and reverence she understood she was meant to be very impressed by the company he kept.

"Polly's very excited about starting this weekend," Rosalind said squinting at the space in front of her, trying to deduce just how many sexy grapes were called for. "She's very passionate about responsible agriculture."

Julian shook his head fiercely, looking up at her work, "I like it."

She worked all afternoon, getting much more done than she'd expected. She hadn't been excited about painting in so long she'd forgotten how quickly the time passed when she was. The grapes were the size of bowling balls; great, sensuous purple orbs joined by strands of deep green, almost black, vines. She would use an iridescent paint over the surface to give it a stained glass effect.

"That's plenty for today," Julian told her, opening a bottle of wine. "Try this," he instructed her.

He held up his own glass to the light and then set it down, swirling it. The ritual of tasting fine wines eluded

Rosalind so she followed his lead. He inhaled the wine deeply, sticking his nose deep within his glass and then set it down again and swirled it some more.

"It's really tight but you'll be amazed how it opens up," he said. He still hadn't tasted it yet, so Rosalind hadn't either. He stuffed his nose back into the glass and stared at it, furrowing his brow, deep in thought as though solving an ancient mystery.

"Blackberries," he said finally. "Do you smell blackberry?"

Rosalind hadn't realized she was supposed to be smelling anything, so she inhaled again.

"Yeah. I do."

But this wasn't enough. He was in search of more smells, he hadn't been satisfied. He inhaled again and stared at the glass accusingly.

"Yes, blackberry. Blackberry and stone fruit. Stone fruit. Stone fruit totally," he said nodding. Finally he tasted it and Rosalind did too. She wondered how long Polly would last in this routine.

"A little tight. Little funky," he said approvingly. "You'll see how much it changes. Maybe we should decant it. You know decanting a wine has the same effect as letting it open for an hour?"

"No kidding."

"Actually, no," he said, putting away the decanter he'd pulled off the bar. "I want you to taste it opening up, it's pretty amazing."

Rosalind wasn't convinced she'd notice the difference, but she kept swirling and smelling and tasting at regular intervals, following Julian.

"You didn't have to work today?" he asked.

Rosalind shook her head.

Julian nodded, sniffed his wine and tasted again. "See? Totally different wine now."

Rosalind smelled and drank. He was right. The taste had mellowed in just the few minutes since her last sip, its character completely transformed into something smoother and richer. The wine was already giving her a slight buzz and she remembered that she had forgotten to eat. She'd been forgetful all day. She kept forgetting she'd cheated on Cal, it disturbed her how often she forgot, as if the past twenty four hours were a life lived by a stranger she had the odd voyeuristic task of observing. She drank again.

"Amazing, right? It just keeps changing," he said.

Rosalind nodded her agreement. "I should get home," she said when he raised the bottle to pour more in her glass.

"Just a splash," he said, refilling her glass. "I don't like to drink alone. Though mind you, I don't make a fetish of it like some people. I used to not drink alone but then I found myself enduring the most tedious company just to enjoy a glass of wine. Present company excluded, of course."

"Thank you."

"Tell me about your husband."

"He's a good person," Rosalind said oddly, as if Julian had suggested he wasn't.

"What does he do?"

"Marketing. Copywriting for this company called DimeEdge."

"I know who they are."

"And he wants to be a writer," she explained.

Julian sighed. "Don't they all?"

"He's very talented," she added in an unexpected fit of loyalty. "He's working on a script about Stalin's pursuit of an ape-man race. It's really good."

"You've read it?"

"Not yet. He hasn't really written it."

Julian smiled, disinterested, turning his attention back to the wine. He inhaled again and sipped, smiling with delight.

Later that night, Rosalind went downstairs to her father's studio with a plan to borrow some of his paint. She wanted to use some of his iridescent colors for Julian's grapes. She found her father still at work. He did that sometimes, working till dawn.

"Didn't know you were here," he said as she entered his studio, not looking away from his work.

"Yeah, just y'know," she said vaguely.

"Cal OK?" he asked, staring at a black painting he was layering over with patches of shimmery silver.

"He's just great," she said so sarcastically that she'd revealed more than she meant to.

Richard cocked an eyebrow, interested now.

"It's nothing," she told him. "I just came in to see about using some of your paint. I'm doing this project for that wine bar guy."

He nodded, waving her toward his paint station. "Take whatever you need."

"I'm trying to get this sort of stained glass effect on these grapes," she explained. "But not too overt. Subtle. Something candlelight would play off of."

"Here's what you want," he said, pointing.

"I just need a little."

"Take the whole thing. Bring back what you don't use."

"OK." She headed for the door and stopped there. "If you could not tell Mom or Polly about Cal and me?"

"What is happening with Cal and you?"

"Just a little… tension. We'll work it out," she lied.

Richard studied her and gave a wry, sad smile.

"You know that poem? *Not waving but drowning?*"

"I'm not drowning and besides people who're drowning don't wave. I read that somewhere."

There was a long pause during which Rosalind tried not to cry.

"You're drowning, aren't you?"

He held her close and she burst into tears.

"There's no shame in it," he said. "We're all drowning sometime."

"He thinks his brother's a dog. That's weird, isn't it?" She had, it seemed, lost all track of what was weird.

Richard thought for a long time as if actually weighing this against every weird thing he had ever heard, nodding with an authoritative finality. "Yeah. That's pretty weird."

They both nodded in agreement and he studied her again.

"What happened?" he asked.

She shook her head. She wasn't going to tell the story of her and Cal. The miscarriage, the depressions, Jordy the dog, the night with Eric. She thought of it all and then dismissed it with huge sigh, shaking her head in a way she hoped seemed self-possessed.

"Nothing. Nothing. It's just hard is all," Rosalind said, regaining her voice, struggling to sound sane.

Richard nodded patiently and then sighed. "A father's only as happy as his unhappiest child."

"Cal and I are probably splitting up," she said, still hedging. Were they splitting up?

Rosalind stood awkwardly, trying not to cry again and failing that, to summon the energy to tell her father she was just fine, really she was. She stood shaking with the effort of holding back more tears. He enfolded her in his arms and she wept quietly.

"It's OK. It'll all be OK. Marriage is the hardest thing. Look how good I am at it," he said.

She managed a faint laugh. "I'll be alright," she assured him.

"Everything's temporary," he said. "Even us. *Especially* us."

It was the kind of darkly existential advice he specialized in. She smiled and noticed how old he looked. He'd been so stoic through his prostate cancer. The disease had officially gone into remission around the time she'd gotten pregnant. He was more delighted than anyone and was stoic again when she miscarried. Was he drowning, not waving?

She gave him a peck on the cheek.

"Are you alright?" she asked, concerned.

"I'm fine. Everything's fine," he said.

She smiled and left, watching him from outside his studio as he moved slowly, deliberately, remembering what he'd been up to before her interruption. It started to rain again and she hurried back inside the house.

nineteen

THE FINAL CLASS OF BEGINNING Tango was poorly attended. It was the last week of August and people were out of town or at the very least in a summer mood, unable to make appointments or attend classes until the sobering fact of Labor Day had passed. A yoga class had occupied the room earlier that day and the air still smelled of sweat and sandalwood incense.

About half a dozen couples moved in slow motion, warming up before class to doleful tango music. Rosalind put on her dance shoes and watched from the sidelines with her mother.

"Shall we?" Helen asked, offering her hand.

Rosalind hated dancing with her mother. Everyone found it adorable.

"OK," Rosalind agreed.

They were fine with the basic step, but as soon as Helen led her into something more complicated the usual trouble began.

"You're supposed to be turning to the left," Helen complained.

"You're supposed to turn me to the left, otherwise I just think you're doing the basic step."

Helen over-corrected, lifting with her right arm and twisting Rosalind.

"Mom, seriously."

"I'm doing it correctly. Here's what you're supposed to do," she said, twisting Rosalind's body further.

"That doesn't even make sense. My body's going this way."

"Well! I'm doing it right. Barry!" Helen said, grabbing his attention. Barry walked towards them, grinning affably. By now he and Mariela treated Helen like a strange aunt, the kind that makes holiday gatherings fractious but more interesting.

"Tell Ros what she's doing wrong," Helen told him. Helen led her into the step, stopping at their usual impasse.

"You need to turn her the other way," he said, taking Rosalind's hand and leading her through the step correctly by way of demonstration.

"Oh, the *other* way!" Helen exclaimed as though Rosalind had not been saying the same thing.

Barry led Rosalind around the floor. She'd danced with him a few times; he was occasionally pressed into service when there was a shortage of men. He had a firm grasp of her back, using his forearm to lift or guide her. She'd heard that an inexperienced follower could dance the tango if the leader had enough skill and she could see how dancing with him. The song ended and the students waited for class to begin. Bethany waved to Helen and stood next to Rosalind.

"Your mom is so cool," Bethany told her. "I'm totally jealous."

Rosalind had been hearing this since high school when her mother would cheerfully drive her teenage friends to the local women's health center for contraceptives or, failing that, abortions. Rosalind just smiled.

"Tonight! We're learning something that's a lot of fun," Mariela told them.

"Ladies," Barry said, "Tonight you get to kick us." This cracked Barry and Mariela up and then once they settled down they clarified. "Well, not really kick us. You're gonna learn a little embellishment called the *gancho*, a kind of kicking motion where the lady hooks her leg under her partner's."

"If you're doing it right, you won't kick your partner," Mariela said. "But it's a place where the ladies — and other followers — get to add a little spice of their own."

Barry and Mariela demonstrated, his left leg clearing a space for Mariela's foot to dart under and out rapidly. They showed variations, all the different places a woman could add "spice" and broke the group into couples. Rosalind ended up with Paul, the man Kev had speculated Helen would be with by the end of the class. He'd been absent a couple of weeks and Rosalind was curious to see them together, to see for herself what Kev had seen between them. Paul was courtly, almost old fashioned, with bright blue eyes and white hair that made him look like a slightly heavy Johnny Carson. Paul danced like he was communicating from a distant planet; he barely held her and was so far away that the *gancho* looked more like an aggressive soccer move.

"Your thigh has to be right up against her thigh," Barry corrected Paul. Paul looked mortified by this news. Barry demonstrated with Rosalind, giving her easy clearance as she kicked up and under his knee.

"See?" Barry asked. Paul nodded and took a deep breath, taking Rosalind's hand.

"Sorry," he said, though it wasn't clear if he was apologizing for not putting his thigh against hers before, or the fact that he was about to, thrusting forward in a lurch. Rosalind clumsily gave a slight kick to the side of his ankle.

"That was good," she assured him. He shook his head and laughed at himself.

"This was my daughter's idea," he said, adding, "This class, I mean."

"You're doing really great," she said, lunging again into a failed *gancho*.

"Maybe we should just practice the basic step?" he suggested.

"That's fine by me."

Paul was sweet and befuddled; Rosalind couldn't quite see the potential for romance Kev had predicted. They moved through the basic step, Paul off in the distance of his own time zone and Rosalind trying to follow.

"It's hard to find a good lead," Mariela whispered to her with a wink as they took their break. Rosalind smiled and nodded.

"Seems to be."

Mariela leaned in confidentially, "My divorce was the best thing that ever happened to me."

Rosalind nodded, uncertain where this was going. "That's great."

"Your mom told me. And what I tell women is 'find a man you can dance with.' I knew the minute I had that first dance with Barry. We just fit and he knew intuitively how to move me."

"My mom told you what?" Rosalind asked, confused.

"About your divorce," she said matter-of-factly.

Rosalind caught sight of her mother across the room, flirting not with Paul but with Kev and Bethany and Andrew, her fan club. Rosalind walked over to her, pulling her aside.

"Mom. What did you tell Mariela about me and Cal?"

"I don't remember," she said.

"Did you tell her I'm getting a divorce?"

"I might have," Helen said, aggrieved at the thought of searching her memory, "I can't remember everything I say."

"I haven't told you I'm getting a divorce — I haven't told anyone."

"Well. Aren't you?"

"It's my *life*," she said, her raised voice attracting attention. People turned to give her a concerned look: *Oh, the poor divorcing dear.* She gathered her sandals and bag and marched outside, walking in her suede-soled dance shoes across pavement even though this was, strictly speaking, not recommended in the care instructions. She got in her car and drove, uncertain of where she was going exactly.

"I wasn't sure if I should call you," Eric said, pouring her a glass of wine. "I mean, I don't really know how these things are done."

"Neither do I," she said defensively.

"I wasn't saying you did. I just meant... I didn't know if you'd want to hear from me."

"No, I know," she said, taking a sip of wine. They were sitting in his living room, a formal space that seemed hardly used. It felt like a retreat of sorts, a move backwards from the intimacy of the breakfast nook and the bedroom.

"I'm glad to see you," he said with a kind of formality that matched the room. He had a large stuffed sofa and two matching leather club chairs that felt fresh from the showroom floor. She took a big gulp of wine. She shouldn't have shown up. He clearly was ready to be done with her and Cal. He probably sat around the teachers' lounge regaling his colleagues with tales of the crazy couple he'd met and how they kept showing up at his house. He looked her over as if puzzled by something.

"Are you wearing dance shoes?"

She'd forgotten about those. She looked down and nodded.

"You're not supposed to wear those outside," he told her.

"I left in kind of a hurry. I should go," she said standing to go.

"What kind of dance?"

"Tango."

"Really?" he asked, looking surprised.

She shrugged. She wasn't about to tell him about Buenos Aires and how it was going to save her marriage and her life. That idea felt like it belonged to another person now. Suddenly he was up, pushing furniture against the wall and rolling up a small area rug.

"Let's see what I remember!" he said.

"Really?" she asked uncertainly.

"I was with this dance company in Germany that incorporated tango into some of their modern pieces. It's been a million years but I'll see what's still there."

It clearly didn't matter what he remembered. He was a dancer. He knew how to hold a frame, how to lead. He held her with exactly the right amount of pressure, moving from open to close embrace, turning her easily, naturally into the next step. He had an assertiveness as a dancer she hadn't seen before, he danced like someone who would burn the house down after his wife left, not preserve her every design choice like a museum. This surprised her. A man usually had a dancing style that captured his personality. But this was a revelation of someone else, someone hidden. Even more certainly than sleeping with him, the dance revealed Eric Ames.

"I'm sorry I didn't call you," he said eventually.

"It's alright."

"I thought about it all the time. It's all I've been thinking about."

"Really?"

As they danced she felt an unraveling. This was where she was supposed to be. She rested her forehead under his chin, making a shelter of him just like the lady in the photo she'd seen, the photo that had started the whole crazy Argentina business.

She danced with her eyes closed. She wasn't sure how much time had passed. There was no music to mark out the three minutes of a song, just the sound of their feet shuffling and dragging and darting. In close embrace there were no secrets — she could feel his heart race and the methodical pulsing of blood as it passed under her thumb at his wrist. They breathed in rhythm, their feet following from the breath, quick and hurried and then slow and deliberate until finally they stood motionless in the middle of the floor, breathing quietly in unison.

"Will you stay the night?" he asked.

Rosalind looked up at him and nodded.

twenty

INGRID INSISTED ON PLAYING THE Smiths that morning. For Rosalind listening to The Smiths was always a short path to suicidal ideation, but Ingrid was adamant. She was back from vacation, tanned and happy, full of pictures and stories and convinced she was "up the duff."

"I swear it, Derek just looks at me when we're in Greece and I'm pregnant. That's how I got Augustus. We tried for years and nothing. You and Cal should try it — I swear, you'd be up the duff by the time you get off the plane."

Rosalind nodded silently; she hadn't told Ingrid anything about the separation from Cal.

"I mean, with the nanny taking care of the kids there's really nothing to do on a Greek island but sun and sleep and drink and have sex. It's perfect. Life should always be like that."

But life was rarely like that even for someone as privileged as Ingrid. Both women stared out the window at the darkening morning clouds, it looked like the makings of a thunderstorm, the air was dry and static. Rosalind jealously contemplated life on a Greek island. She imagined going there with Eric, spending long days doing nothing but watching the sun rise, traverse a cloudless sky, and set. From the iPod Morrissey plaintively begged to *please, please, please let me get what I want, Lord knows, it would be the first time…*

"Jesus, Ingrid —" Rosalind said, turning off the song.

"Oh!" Ingrid made a comic face of disappointment. "I love him. I don't know what it is but when I'm pregnant I just want to listen to the saddest songs and hear the funniest jokes and just live, live, live! Like *everything's* so intense. I *love* being pregnant so much."

Rosalind mustered a tight supportive smile.

"I'm sorry, God, that was insensitive," Ingrid said. "Are you and Cal still trying?"

"Yeah."

Rosalind wasn't in the mood to share what was going on. Ingrid nodded sympathetically and reached out to stroke Rosalind's hair. This was precisely why Rosalind avoided telling her anything: all that smug, pregnant-lady sympathy. She knew Ingrid meant well but she only made things worse. Rosalind busied herself with some bookkeeping, going over the numbers for the weeks Ingrid was gone. She thought to ask about a raise. If she and Cal really were finished she'd need it. But Ingrid started complaining about the landlord and how her lease was up soon and she hadn't gotten any sense of how much he'd be asking to renew.

"This whole neighborhood's gone crazy," she said, exasperated. "I don't know if we're even going to be able to afford to stay here."

Rosalind nodded. She'd ask for a raise some other time.

"Anything else happen while I was gone?"

"Oh, yeah," Rosalind remembered, "There's this woman trying to return a blanket we don't carry —"

Ingrid laughed. "My voicemail was full. I swear," Ingrid said, shaking her head sadly — dreaming, no doubt, of her Greek isle — "one of these days I've gotta find a business that doesn't involve catering to bitches."

Rosalind continued painting the sexy grapes using the silver paint from her father. She worried the grapes were becoming too beautiful, not like Cezanne's apples that Rilke had described as neither pretty nor ugly but simply good for cooking. Maybe the silver paint was too much?

"Luminous," Julian said, glaring at the wall. "I love it." He moved behind the bar, opening a bottle of sparkling wine. "Let's celebrate," he said, thrusting a glass into her hand and holding his drink up to toast the freshly painted wall.

It had come out well. Better than she had expected. The silver accents picked up the light in a way that drew the eye up and into the tangle of grapes. Julian walked the four doors down and persuaded Ingrid to close her store long enough to admire the grapes as well.

"This is what I love about Portland!" he said, pouring more wine, "everyone has something else going on, some other talent they're nurturing. You can walk down your block and find a great artist working behind some counter."

"Please," Rosalind demurred, embarrassed.

"You are. You are!" insisted Julian. "Isn't she, Ingrid?"

"She's very talented," Ingrid agreed. "No more for me," she said, putting her hand over the glass. "Bun in the oven!"

Rosalind felt a familiar twinge of jealous sadness but Julian looked indifferently at Ingrid — he had nothing to say about pregnancy — and turned back to Rosalind, "You should have a show! Isn't that what people do?"

"People who have paintings to actually show," Rosalind managed. She could maybe accept being the woman who gave up family for a career but to be closing in on forty with neither? It seemed like very poor planning.

"You have paintings," Ingrid said.

"I have *hummingbirds*," Rosalind corrected.

"You are an artist," he said.

"I'm a clerk with pretensions, that's it," Rosalind countered.

"That's a horrible thing to think! I am getting you commissions off this. Mark my words!" he said, finishing his wine with dramatic flourish.

Rosalind smiled and stared out the window. The sky was a piercing shade of blue, the kind that lingered on her retinas after she shut her eyes. It was the type of sunny autumn day that made people pack up their belongings and move to the Northwest in the first place. The air was crisp and people strode purposelessly, briefly convinced that no other kind of day existed. November would soon land with a gray thud leaving the inhabitants to recall this afternoon wistfully, returning in their memories to the day that made eight months of overcast skies endurable.

Her cell phone rang. It was Eric.

"Cal called me," he said.

Rosalind excused herself and stepped outside.

"What? Why?"

"He really misses Jordy and says since we're together he should get the dog."

"I hope you hung up on him," she said, stung. Why wasn't Cal fighting for *her*?

"No," Eric admitted hesitantly, "I said that would be fine."

"You're exchanging me for a dog? *For a dog.*"

"Actually, technically, Cal is," he said, perhaps now realizing how it all sounded.

"I have to go," she said.

She hung up and walked down the street of trendy bars with people dining outside, enjoying the sun. Choruses of delighted people ordered plates and pitchers while Rosalind tuned them out, focusing on what had suddenly become the most vital question: who was worse, the man who offers you in exchange for a dog or the one who accepts?

She'd fallen for Eric Ames. But what did that mean? How could she love someone she barely knew? A year ago she would have said it was impossible: love was a choice people made daily and longevity was its measure. Love did not crash-land in your living room leaving you squinting into daylight, picking through the debris of your former life. Only now could she see it was sometimes a phantom thing, a stray that wandered the periphery of your life and moved in the minute you opened the door for who knew for how long? The thought of not returning to Eric that night was physically painful. When she went to his house he was kind and apologetic, the furniture had been pushed against the wall and dinner had been made.

"After Janine I guess I'm a little paranoid. I guess, in my head, I heard there was an exchange and then I'd be safe. He couldn't take you back. You would stay."

Rosalind nodded. She looked all around her. She was surrounded by Janine. "Maybe we could paint the walls someday," she suggested.

"What's wrong with them?"

"It doesn't feel like their ours."

Eric nodded as if he understood. They danced that night — as they often did. She resolved to be happy while she could, moving backwards in an eternal circle around his living room.

They didn't talk the way new lovers often do, sharing everything; they were selective and wary. Sometimes it seemed to her their relationship was mostly physical, something she enjoyed. She purchased expensive lingerie that, in her Cal days of utilitarian cotton, would have been unthinkable; she would have felt ridiculous. Now she slapped down a credit card and bought sets in pink and lavender and black and red. She laid them out on the bed and told Eric to pick the pair she should wear before they went out dancing. He could think about her wearing them and then peel them off her when they got home.

"You know what we have?" he asked on such a night, lying next to her and circling her breast with a finger. Rosalind's new lingerie— a pink and black lace number that Eric had especially liked — rested in a heap in the corner.

"What?"

"We have the perfect life," he said.

Rosalind laughed then realized he wasn't joking. He had a way of expressing himself dramatically that she often first took as humor.

"It's true. Everything about our lives is perfect," he said.

"Perfect for you," she said. "You like your job."

"That's true. We have to find you a job you like."

"I have to start painting more is what I need to do."

"You could paint here," he told her.

"All my paints are at my house. My *old* house," she corrected herself.

"But other than that — things are perfect aren't they?" he asked again needing, it seemed, corroboration.

Rosalind smiled. "Yes, they're perfect."

twenty one

"I FELL INTO THE trap of essentialism. Me! Can you believe it?"

"Hi, Mom," Rosalind said.

It was a typical pattern with her mother, weeks of silence followed by a phone call full of non-sequiturs. Rosalind was on a lunch break from *little fig*, reading a magazine in a cafe while quickly downing a cup of soup.

"I totally fell in with this notion that followers were passive, feminine. But there's a whole study of follower subversion. Are you aware of it?"

"Of course not."

"It's fascinating. There's a whole school of feminist thought regarding following in tango. And did you know the Jews were into tango? I mean it makes sense when you listen to the music, there are obvious influences going back and forth. Here's an ugly bit of history: the Nazis would force musicians and dancers to perform tangos in the camps in order to survive. I swear it's like there's no group that didn't somehow end up influencing or being influenced by tango. It's huge in Japan and Finland and Turkey — it's everywhere!"

"Mom. I don't have a lot of time."

"Are you still mad at me? Over that little thing?"

"It's not a little thing."

There was a long silence at the other end of the phone.

"Well. Suit yourself. Be mad if you want. I just called to tell you I've signed you up for the intermediate course."

"Mom, I wish you hadn't. I'm really strapped right now —"

"I paid for it myself. No arguments. And. We're all going to our first *milonga* this weekend and you should come — you're a better dancer than any of us. It's Andrew's birthday."

"I have a lot going on."

"Rosalind. Alright. I'm sorry. I shouldn't have spoken out of turn. Will you please join us?" A real apology was a rare thing out of her mother even with the hasty, exasperated tone.

"I'll think about it," she said, but she knew already she would go.

On the night of the *milonga* Rosalind suspected there would be a battle. Eric still hadn't met any of her family. She had deliberately kept them separate.

"Why hide me?" he asked.

"It's not *you* I'm hiding, believe me."

"How bad can they be?"

Rosalind hesitated. "I just don't think tonight's the night. I'm still not on great terms with my mom."

He finally relented and he went alone, driving downtown to a club that hosted *milongas* twice a month. It was a large old dancehall with ornate moldings and columns bordering a small stage where, in a pool of red light, a bandoneon player and pianist pounded out a tango in a hard, driving rhythm. The room was dimly lit, with a dance floor ringed by tables where women sat alone or in pairs waiting to be asked to dance and men trolled the periphery silently asking with a slight bow of the head. She felt like she had wandered into another country and warily changed into her dance shoes, watching from the sidelines, recognizing with relief a familiar face amongst the dancers: Andrew. A hive of grave looking couples moved in a great meandering circle that appeared to swell and retract as though being breathed. The dancers moved elegantly, deliberately in terrifying unison.

Rosalind watched Andrew smile nervously, clearly flummoxed by the large woman with short dark hair he was coaxing around the room. The woman danced with an economy of motion Rosalind had noted among the very talented. There was always something self-contained about the better dancers; they held something in reserve, a restraint formed mysteriously by something they'd given up opposing. This surrender made the dancers beautiful. Rosalind had noticed it from the first, the way that skill reordered things; skill altered the economy of beauty so that this woman with a face like an old spoon would be the one men wanted to dance with all night. The dance and her skill at it made her desirable. She moved with a calm dignity as though it had never occurred to her that someone wouldn't want to dance with her. The music ended. The woman gave Andrew a tight smile.

Andrew moved to Rosalind, smiling for her benefit.

"You looked good out there," she told him.

"That lady scares the bejesus out of me."

Rosalind laughed lightly and nodded, moving on to the floor with him. They moved easily around the floor. Andrew wasn't one for anything complicated and

Rosalind was grateful for that. He stuck to the simplest of steps, leading her without much effort.

"Is Kev here?" she asked.

He gave a grim little shake of his head to indicate that he didn't care to discuss it any further. She nodded and they moved silently, both preoccupied with their own little dramas, both a little too detached to care if they sometimes moved wrong or bumped into another couple. They walked and turned. Occasionally Andrew would put out his foot for Rosalind to draw her own foot flirtatiously up his leg. The lack of sexual attraction made a dance of sexual attraction strangely easier. The ritual felt comfortable and a little silly. The song ended. Now Andrew and Rosalind together made a great show of standing on the edges of the room, affecting confidence in a sea of more talented dancers as everyone sought out new partners. Andrew gave an involuntary sigh.

"You wanna get a drink?"

Rosalind nodded and followed him to the bar, which had a separate lounge in view of the dance floor. She had never really gotten to know Andrew. Helen had befriended him straightaway and kept a running report on his fledgling romance with Kev. Rosalind knew her mother disapproved of the match, believing Andrew too sensitive and bookish for the glamorous Kev and predicting it would end in tears. They ordered drinks and sat quietly in a kind of mutual embarrassment that they hadn't ever really gotten to know each other.

"My mom's usually really punctual. I wonder where she is," Rosalind observed.

"Kev's never on time," Andrew said gloomily.

Rosalind searched her mind. She could not find a single thing to say to Andrew as he stared into the crowd of dancers with a look of weary resignation.

"Are you taking the intermediate class?" Rosalind asked finally.

Andrew nodded.

They watched the dancers, admired the musicians. They smiled at each other and drank. Rosalind had nearly finished her glass of wine when a gentlemen in a well-pressed suit bowed into her eyesight, offering his hand. She'd thought they were far enough away from the dance floor that no one would ask her to dance. He was in his late forties, olive-skinned, Persian maybe, and had a formality and correctness that was intimidating. Rosalind smiled and took his hand, following him to the floor.

"I'm a beginner," she whispered as he wrapped an arm around her back in close embrace. He nodded, apparently unworried by this news and led her carefully around the floor. He was an expert, which made her more self-conscious.

"You're better than a beginner," he said in a way that was half sincere and half patronizing.

"Famous last words," she said, smiling and feeling a wellspring of irritation that she'd come at all. He noticed her looking at her feet.

"Don't worry about your feet. There are no steps. Just follow me," he told her.

Rosalind tried but couldn't fight the compulsion to find the right steps.

"No steps!" he told her again, now clearly a bit irritated with her.

"Sorry. That's how I learned," Rosalind shot back testily.

"You shouldn't be learning steps. That is not real tango," he informed her solemnly.

"That's what I hear."

Miraculously the dance ended. She thanked him, he thanked her and she returned to the table. She hadn't believed it was possible for the conversation with Andrew to be more strained than it was until Paul showed up. Rosalind hadn't expected to see him. Now three people sat around a tiny table pretending not to be searching for a topic of conversation.

"Are you taking the intermediate class?" Rosalind asked Paul. He smoothed a hand over his white hair as though coming to a decision that minute. "I might. You?"

"My mom signed me up," she said.

"Where *is* Helen?" Paul asked and she could tell from his expression that Kev was right, there was something going on.

"I don't know. She's usually very punctual."

"That's true," he agreed.

"Holy shit, how late are we?" Kev asked, pulling up chairs with Bethany and Helen in a wave of commotion. The act of sitting down caused Kev to break into peals of laughter. Bethany quickly joined him.

"We totally just dropped some E over at Bethany's," he told them.

Andrew rolled his eyes. Paul watched on, confused.

"I asked you not to," Andrew told them pointedly.

"Are you turning ninety or twenty-eight? Good lord. Relax," Kev said.

"I asked you not to be fucked up tonight," Andrew snapped.

Helen turned to Rosalind, noticing her. "Oh honey, you came after all."

"Mom, you're —"

"Oh, God no. Although I did a little —" she made a toking gesture which made Kev and Bethany dissolve into laughter.

"I love your mother," Kev told her.

"I love her more," Bethany said, taking a look around. "Awwwesome! This place is great."

"It's like we're not in America," Kev observed.

"D'you know how cool it would be if we were somewhere else right now?" Bethany asked.

"I know, right?" Kev agreed.

Andrew glared at the two of them.

"You can't be angry on your birthday, Andrew. Let me get you a drink," Helen said.

Paul rose, suddenly finding something he could understand. "I'll get us all a round," he said. "What would anybody like?"

"A man from the IRS is here for Rosalind," Kev said, his voice full of apprehension. Rosalind turned with surprise to see Eric standing over her, offering a dance. The entire table watched her as a new song began. She stared at him, taking his hand. They walked out to the floor together.

"We agreed you weren't coming," she said as they began to dance.

"I want to meet your family, Ros."

"Trust me, you really don't. Not tonight."

"How much do they know about me?"

"I haven't really talked to anyone lately," she admitted.

"No one knows?" he asked, surprised.

"I wanted to pick the right moment. This isn't it," she told him.

"I want them to know about me."

"They will," she promised, she could feel the eyes of her mother and their friends on them, watching their dance, by now intrigued she was having a serious conversation with someone they believed to be a stranger. He turned her forward and back, dancing with a methodical and steady gait, pushing her back and back and back and then holding her as her foot described a half circle on the floor and then traced the outside of his leg. He pulled her into him as the song ended and kissed her.

"I want them to know who I am," he whispered dramatically.

"Well. Mission accomplished."

They walked back to the table together. Kev stood and clapped dramatically.

"Holy shit. I think I came just watching you two!" he said, shaking hands with Eric in congratulations.

"Don't be gross!" Bethany said, slapping Kev playfully.

"We are totally making out together later," Kev told Eric. Eric smiled agreeably, unsure how to respond.

"Eric, this is my mother, Helen," Rosalind said as the two faced each other. Helen looked him over with an expression somewhere between bewildered and delighted.

"Eric is my friend," she said. "Well, lover, actually."

"I *hope* so," Kev said.

"We're also living together," Eric added.

A look passed between mother and daughter, a communication ancient and precise: *we'll talk about it later.*

Eric was invited to sit. Drinks were passed around and various stages of intoxication were negotiated amongst the party. Andrew was coaxed out of his foul mood and Helen kept them all entertained with a story about one of her latest classes.

"I wish I knew stuff like you do, Helen. That is *so* coooool," Bethany said.

"She does know stuff," Kev agreed, studying Helen closely, "like so much stuff it's like your head should just be twice as big. Arghhh! Let's dance! C'mon."

Kev and Bethany headed towards the floor and Rosalind turned her head from what was sure to be a disaster.

Helen and Paul. Rosalind and Eric. And Andrew. They all eyed each other with various degrees of hesitation.

"How long have you known Rosalind?" Helen asked Eric.

"A while," Eric said, a satisfied smile spreading across his face.

"Can I get anyone anything from the bar?" Rosalind asked, irritated by both of them.

"Sit, I'll go," Eric told her.

"No. Don't," she said hastily and left. Helen followed her to the bar.

"He seems wonderful. Very sexy," she told Rosalind.

"Red wine, please," Rosalind asked the bartender.

"I'll have a white wine," Helen told him. They stood awkwardly waiting for their drinks in silence. It was unlike Helen to leave the air unfilled with chatter. When their drinks finally arrived they moved from the bar and Helen gestured for Rosalind to join her at an isolated table.

"I know I've upset you" Helen admitted. She gestured again for Rosalind to pull up a chair. "I will tell you something that nobody knows and then you will always have it over me."

Rosalind sat down, intrigued. Helen leaned across the table confidentially, "I haven't had sex in over twenty years."

Rosalind nodded, unsure what to say.

"I know, me, *me!* — I should be getting laid all the time. Nothing. I mean, it wasn't deliberate or anything. It's not like you get out of bed after the last time and say, 'OK, that's it, I'm done.' It was gradual. Not gradual. It just stopped happening and I stopped pursuing it and then finally a year passes and you think, 'oh, a year' and then ten years and then you just give up. You give up on yourself."

This last bit of information seemed to be a realization for Helen as well. She watched the couples moving to a joyous, playful tango.

"Anyway, there it is."

"Why are you telling me?" Rosalind asked.

"I don't want you to be mad at me anymore."

She gave Helen a disbelieving look.

"I've been mad at you before."

Helen shrugged, searching her mind to find her true motivation.

"I guess I see you and I'm inspired! Life's knocked you down and what do you do? You give it another go! You dare to get hurt again because you're alive. I let myself turn inward and just...stop. When Richard stopped loving me, I just stopped and I didn't even realize it until recently."

Rosalind could see tears in her mother's eyes.

"I'm sorry," Rosalind said. "So. *Are* you with Paul?"

"No, of course not!"

"Why *of course not?*"

Helen considered the possibility, an edge of excitement in her voice as she offered the only negative she could think of: "He did vote for Romney."

The formal Persian man Rosalind had danced with earlier bent in to her ear.

"Your friends are —"

"Oh, Kev!" Rosalind remembered. "He crashes into people, I know."

"They're not really crashing," he said, gesturing to Kev and Bethany where they stood in the center of the dance floor hugging each other.

"We'll take care of them," Rosalind assured him.

"This is traditional *milonga*," he warned her sternly.

The party moved to the Plumley house where Helen unwisely put on some Portuguese *fado* music, whose sad wailing instantly made everyone morose and nostalgic. Paul easily worked himself to a state of misty-eyed grief over his wife Bridget who'd died four years earlier from cervical cancer. Andrew bemoaned his fate as an underpaid grant writer for a non-profit, while Helen repeatedly returned to the stereo with something new everyone had to listen to. Kev and Bethany retired to the backyard where Rosalind could hear they'd discovered the swing set.

"I'll tell Dad," Rosalind announced, in case he was in his studio and wondered why drugged strangers were playing in his backyard.

"He's out," Helen told her, her attention fixed on the liner notes of a CD.

"Really? Where?"

Helen shrugged. "He's been spending a lot of nights out lately."

Rosalind looked to her for elaboration.

"Here it is!" she cried, finding what she was looking for. "It's some kind of new tango," she explained. She put on heavily synthesized, techno-sounding tango music and pulled Paul into a dance. Rosalind watched them. They were both terrible dancers but there was something poignant about the way they negotiated their way around the room, Helen correcting his lead, arguing and then falling into a few comfortable steps. They were shy and awkward together and — was it possible? — her mother actually seemed cute.

Polly showed up with a couple bottles of wine from *Terroir*.

"You're still working there?" Rosalind asked, amazed.

"Uh. Yeah. Why wouldn't I?" Polly asked, studying Eric, who had a proprietary arm around Rosalind's waist. Polly poured wine, describing its qualities with surprising competence. She had, Rosalind realized, finally found an employable expression of her bossiness and sense of superiority.

"This one is from this amaaaazing vineyard up in Washington. Totally organic and when you taste it — taste it," she commanded everyone, "you can taste a kind of mineral quality? That's old volcanic residue. How cool, right?"

The second bottle was less impressive. Polly noted it had an interesting taste of pencil shavings, but was still unstructured and needed more time to mature. The party nodded seriously, wondering if that maturity would occur soon enough for them to finish the bottle that night.

"How is it two a.m.?" Bethany yelled from the kitchen. She and Kev had come inside. "It was just ten!"

Bethany and Kev sat on a sofa listening to techno tango, swaying, entranced by its rhythm. Andrew drank whiskey and pulled Kev up to dance. Before long Kev and Andrew were making out on the dance floor and Paul was making noises about leaving.

"You can't leave now," Helen told him.

"We should get doughnuts!" cried Bethany.

Rosalind noticed her mother was fluttery and nervous, downing her wine in great gulps. Paul smiled at Helen and then looked dramatically at his watch.

"I really should go," he told her.

"One more dance," she insisted, returning the music to a tango. He agreed and they moved stiffly around the floor. The front door swung open and Rosalind turned to see her father watching the scene unfold.

"Hi," Rosalind said uncomfortably.

Richard nodded. Helen stopped dancing briefly.

"Richard, we're dancing the tango," she told him unnecessarily.

He nodded and they stared at each other and then, deciding for both of them, Helen returned to the dance.

"G'night," was all Richard said before he stalked out to his studio. Helen stopped the dance suddenly.

"Alright. Who wants eggs?" she asked.

Paul shook his head, searching for his coat in a pile on one of the couches. "I'll see you at the next class," he said, bowing slightly at the waist.

After he left, the party fractured. Polly and Bethany talked about the dearth of good, available, straight men in town and, as if to illustrate the point, Kev and Andrew occupied the other couch making out. Helen discussed public schools with Eric in the kitchen, whipping up an omelet.

"I know charter schools have had their successes but I just will never part with the public school system.

twenty two

OCTOBER PASSED AS ONE LONG rainy afternoon. In November, the skies darkened to a deep slate by 4:30 and Rosalind drove home each night from *little fig* in what felt like an endless gale. At times it seemed like the whole city had been sunk underwater like an old shipwreck buffeted by tidal currents. She was certain the hair at the nape of her neck hadn't been fully dry since sometime in late September. She was still getting used to her life, still getting used to Eric Ames. He was guileless and given to emotional displays, he could say things like, "we've always been together" in complete seriousness and she wouldn't even smirk at the melodrama of it. She felt what it meant to be "swept away," the words literally true, whatever her former life looked like, whoever she was had shifted.

But it wasn't long before she stopped being mad at Cal and started to worry. Trading a woman for a dog wasn't Cal. At least the Cal she had known. He arranged to be gone during her many visits to the house to pack her things. She thought to surprise him at home, showing up unannounced to check up on him, but she only surprised Glen, sitting on the couch watching *The Rockford Files*. The house had taken on a funky, opium den quality.

"Hey, Cal's not around?" she asked casually.

"Naw. Sorry about you guys. You were cool together," Glen mustered before returning his attention to Jim Rockford.

"You don't know when he's coming back?"

"No."

"Is he OK?"

"Like how?"

"Y'know, how's he doing?"

"Y'mean his mental state?" Glen asked.

"Yeah, I do. Is he alright?"

Glen gave this a second's consideration.

"Guess so," he reasoned. "I mean, what's 'alright,' anyway, right?"

Not trading women for dogs, for starters, Rosalind thought. She nodded uneasily. No more insights would be forthcoming.

"Thanks, Glen."

"Hey. Take it easy."

She tried checking the *DimeEdge* web site, struggling to discern from the ad-copy he wrote how he was doing. Was the description of a fleece-lined Gore-Tex parka as an "embrace of warmth and comfort that shields against the coldest night" a cry for help or the happy ramblings of a man who'd just made the best trade of his life?

Rosalind picked up Hermione and Laurent in front of the airport. The perpetual drizzle of the past week had finally let up and she found them huddled together, waving to her in excitement. As she pulled up, Laurent flew into action, a crazy profusion of bags and rolling suitcases appeared from beneath them which he quickly hurled into the trunk Rosalind had just opened for him.

Introductions could wait. Hermione tried to lift a tiny overnight satchel.

"Non!" he told her, waving her away, tucking the satchel expertly between two larger pieces.

"Look at you!" Rosalind exclaimed. Her sister looked enormous and gorgeous and happy. Rosalind felt a pang of grief and smiled.

Hermione rolled her eyes, embracing her sister. "I know. I'm huge."

"Hello!" Laurent said brightly, taking Rosalind's hand.

"Hi! It's so nice to meet you."

"It is very nice to meet you too," he said, bowing his head slightly. He was shorter than Hermione, stout and soft, wearing a navy blue parka and tan slacks. He looked every bit the cheerful and reliable rescuer of Hermione's story. He gazed at Hermione like she was a glittering prize. Rosalind imagined him staying up nights with his unmarried male friends, pointing to his wife as evidence that nice guys really do sometimes get the girl.

They climbed into Rosalind's car, Hermione up front and Laurent in the back.

"How was your flight?"

Hermione and Laurent agreed it had been just fine.

"How're mom and dad?" Hermione asked.

"Fine. The same."

"Are you and Cal still…?"

"Yeah. We're separated. Officially."

"What's going on?"

"It's… a long story." She looked in her rearview mirror to gauge Laurent's reaction but he was already busy checking e-mails on his phone.

"Or a short story, I guess," she told Hermione. "I'm with someone else."

Hermione gasped. "You had an affair?"

"No. Not really. Sort of. No. We'll talk about it later."

"But I like Cal!"

Rosalind nodded, not wanting to talk about it. "Mom's very curious about your secret."

"You haven't told her yet?" Hermione asked.

Rosalind shook her head — she and her father were the only Plumleys who could keep a secret.

"She did say she hoped Anton hadn't gotten you knocked up." Rosalind said. Hermione snorted.

"As if pregnancy was the biggest tragedy of a woman's life. I'm 39! How much longer would she like me to wait?"

Rosalind nodded agreement, her eyes on the road.

"I really am sorry about Cal," Hermione said, squeezing Rosalind's knee. "I know it must be tough."

"Yeah," Rosalind agreed and forced a smile.

When they arrived at the house, Laurent unloaded the trunk with the same efficiency with which he'd loaded it. The front door was already open with Helen waiting in anticipation, glass of wine already in hand; some premonition clearly told her she'd need wine.

"My baby!" she cried, pulling Hermione into a tight embrace. "Look at how beautiful you are! Women are so beautiful when they're pregnant. I just knew it!"

"You're happy?" Hermione asked, incredulous.

"Of course I am! I mean, babies ruin your life but —" she gave a large expansive wave of her arm "— then they grow up! Let me get Richard. Richard!" Helen stalked off in the direction of the studio while Laurent dutifully lugged suitcases from the curb. Rosalind and Hermione shared a look of surprise.

"Well. You can still disappoint her with your job and the house in the suburbs," Rosalind joked.

Richard and Polly were collected from the far corners of the house. Laurent was introduced and talk of due dates and baby names ("February" "It's a girl!") and sonograms and a brief obligatory discourse on the superiority of the French health care system consumed another tense thirty minutes before Hermione finally took a deep breath and blurted out the whole ugly truth of her existence.

"I hate theater. I've been working in Human Resources for Genoco Pharmaceuticals for four years. We live twenty minutes outside Paris in a suburb. Laurent programs software. We're married. And we want a real turkey for Thanksgiving."

Richard absorbed this news with his usual calm amusement. Helen leaned away as though blown back by it all.

"Well," she said, blinking at the two of them. She took a sip of her wine, choosing what to say. "You know how Polly feels about turkey."

"And Genoco is totally corrupt," Polly said, storming from the room.

"Hermione," Helen began calmly, "We're happy for you both. But Genoco *and* turkey? You have to space these things out. Think of Polly."

"Oh my God, are you serious? All we do is tiptoe around Polly's moods. She's a grown-up. She can have her veggie casserole but this is Laurent's first Thanksgiving and we didn't fly halfway across the world just to eat some *fucking eggplant*?"

"Is OK," Laurent said, rubbing his wife's shoulders.

"No, it's not. Polly is a little brat and we all have to dance to her tune. Why do you think I stay away so much?" Hermione asked.

"That's not entirely fair," Rosalind responded. "Polly's a lot of things, but she's not the only reason you've stayed away." A look passed between the two sisters as the room fell silent.

"I'm with Hermione. I'd like a turkey too," Richard said, wading into the silence. "It'd be nice." He gave a look of grudging acceptance to Helen. "C'mon," he said to her. "It's the last one."

"It's the what?" Hermione asked, picking up on those words in a way only a child — even an adult one — could.

Helen sighed and gave Richard a look of eternal irritation.

"Do you want to tell them?" she asked.

"I think I just did."

"Fine. Fine. Your father and I are getting a divorce. He's qualifies for Medicare and he's in love with a potter named Katherine."

"Ceramicist," Richard corrected.

"Ceramicist," Helen repeated.

To Rosalind it all made sense, but Hermione stared at them, horrified.

"You can't get divorced. I'm having a baby! How can you do this to me right now?" Hermione asked, tears welling in her eyes. Laurent whispered in her ear, soothing words in French. They exchanged more words in French, a brief, minor argument.

"I think it's been a long day for us," Laurent said with grand understatement. "I think maybe we lie down?" Hermione led him upstairs.

Helen looked disapprovingly at Richard.

"We could've told them later."

Richard raised his hands in exasperation. "They're in their *thirties*."

"It's a big deal, Richard. You do no one any favors by minimizing or invalidating their emotional response," Helen snapped. She left for the kitchen where she poured herself more wine. Richard looked at Rosalind who had been sitting this whole time in an overstuffed chair marveling at the drama unfolding before her.

Richard sighed, his eyes surveying the near empty room as if trying to memorize it for future reference.

"So. You want to make a turkey?" he finally asked her. He always had a way of getting back to the basics.

Rosalind nodded her head, still a little stunned.

"Sure," she said finally. "Why not?"

twenty three

HERMIONE FINALLY EMERGED THE NEXT day determined to buy a turkey. She and Rosalind lingered over the confusing array at the grocery store.

"Definitely no hormones," Hermione said.

"Organic," Rosalind read off the label, "no hormones, free range —"

"Perfect! I'm gonna go find yams. Laurent loves yams." Hermione left as Rosalind hoisted their turkey into her cart, noticing a woman about Rosalind's age, very pregnant with a six-year-old girl by her side. Holy sweet Jesus, she thought, was anyone *not* pregnant? The woman was equally perplexed by the vast selection. Rosalind gave her a sympathetic look.

"Hard to remember what to be afraid of," Rosalind said.

"Right?"

The woman's daughter wore blue jeans and a pirate's hat, a makeshift wooden sword tucked into her belt-loops. She had devised a routine of rotating her body so that the sword made a pleasing *thwack!* sound against her mother's calf.

"Honey, please don't do that. That doesn't make Mommy's leg feel good."

Thwack, thwack, thwack.

"Olive! Please."

Rosalind gave the woman an understanding smile as she turned her cart around.

"You look really familiar," the woman said, stopping her. Rosalind looked at her — she seemed familiar as well. She had dark red hair pulled back in a ponytail.

"Oh, my God. What's your name?"

"Rosalind Plumley."

"Oh, my God, yes! Olive, stop! Lucinda," she said, placing a hand on her chest. "I was Lucinda Greene. Now I'm Posen."

"OK. Yeah. How've you been?"

"Oh, you know," she said, lifting a fatigued hand over her daughter and her pregnant belly.

"She's very sweet," Rosalind told her.

"She hasn't changed out of her Halloween costume in three weeks. I have no idea how I'm going to get her into a dress tomorrow."

"I'm'a go home," the girl announced, her boredom making the thwacks more pronounced.

"In a minute, honey," Lucinda said. "It's our first Thanksgiving back in Portland in, like, forever. My husband's from back east and we've been in New York for the past, God! ten years."

Rosalind nodded. "You look great."

Lucinda sighed. "Thanks. You too! What's going on? I remember you were so *talented*."

"Thanks."

"I remember in high school thinking you were this supercool chick who'd end up in Paris or something really awesome like that."

"Nope. Still here."

"Still painting?"

"Here and there."

Lucinda smiled intensely. "I was in graphic design until Olive. We just moved back. My husband got a job at Wieden."

"Wow. That's great."

"Yeaaaah. We're good. So! Good to see you and maybe sometime…"

"We can get a coffee," Rosalind finished her thought. "There's lots of great places."

"I know, right? So much cooler than when we were growing up!" Lucinda said.

"I was in New York actually. For a while," Rosalind suddenly felt it was necessary to inform her.

"No, kidding! Didn't you love it?'

"Yeah. I wasn't there long but, y'know, it's great. I mean, it's New York, right?"

"Tell me about it. I love being back but there's not a day goes by I don't miss it."

Rosalind pretended to agree. They agreed to meet again, a plan they both knew they'd never keep. Filling the trunk with groceries while the pregnant Hermione waited in the passenger seat, Rosalind felt a stab of sadness. Ever since she and Cal split, Rosalind had nurtured a new thought: she would never have children. She wasn't sure what to feel about it, or rather, she felt an odd premonition of regret, a nostalgia for something she didn't yet miss. Seeing Lucinda made her think what might have been had she stayed in New York. Would she have married a successful ad-man and been able to rush around town with an eccentric daughter?

Every choice contained its opposite. It was impossible not to wonder what life would have been like if she'd only altered one stray thread of it. One by one her friends had all started having children and then fell out of her life, appearing, if at all, in quarterly installments like business taxes. She missed her friends. They showed up for elaborately negotiated nights out, haggard and worn, their eyes distant and haunted as if they'd just appeared in a Bergman film, recounting devastated sex lives and years of sleep missed and then stare deep in her eyes and say, "you really gotta do it — it's like you don't know what love is until you have a kid." Then they'd drink half a bottle of light beer and insist they had to be home by 9 o'clock. They hadn't seen a non-Disney film in over five years. They didn't read books anymore. If they knew who Wes Anderson was it was only because of that film with the foxes. And the horrible thing was: what if they were right? What if she lived her whole life and never really knew what love was? What if it was deeper than she'd ever imagined? What if she died without ever knowing what she'd missed? How would she know to even miss it? Love — deep, profound, soul-stirring love — happened on this planet, in this life. And she'd missed it.

On the other hand, her mother had a point: babies were awful. They were selfish, greedy, expensive and ultimately resentful of what they later would decide you had withheld from them. You were, in effect, creating someone uniquely fine-tuned to discern your slightest faults and broadcast them from the highest point. Rosalind was well acquainted with arguments both for and against. When she was pregnant she couldn't help but worry about what she was giving up and what dire responsibilities she would prove unfit for. When she miscarried all she could think of was what she would never know. Babies didn't excite her but the thought of a precocious nine-year-old, half her, half Cal, some enchanting being she could share lunches and museums and movies with, all the while devising preposterous theories to explain the world? Well, now. That would be something.

And who would advocate for her? Who would arrange her doctor appointments and throw out rotting bananas as she drifted into old age? Who would keep her photos, her jewelry, her horrible shadowboxes full of undergraduate angst, her hummingbird paintings or even her tango shoes? Who would care about all the random junk she'd accumulated over the years and the stories that had attached to them? All those family photos at a sad estate sale? Free to be picked over by any weirdo looking for ironically nostalgic family photos for a new bar in some snide, emotionally cruel future Portland? She realized children shouldn't be thought of as mere post-mortem media storage sites but really, where on earth was she going to unload all her earthly crap if not upon someone biologically required to care? The Lucindas of the world were taken care of. Forty years from now Olive would be cleaning out her mother's basement and making sure her many medications weren't contraindicated. Rosalind? Who would care?

twenty four

"YOU TALKED TO A lawyer yet?" Hermione asked as they prepared the turkey. Rosalind shook her head, her hands deep inside the turkey's cavity. In fact, she was very actively trying not to think about it. Divorce. Lawyers. It was all so grown up and unreal to her.

"Eric liked his guy so I might go with him. I'll deal with it later."

"Have you and Cal seen a therapist? Or a mediator?" Rosalind shook her head.

"Cause you and Cal go way back. You have a lot of history together," Hermione said.

"So do France and Germany," Rosalind replied tersely.

"I'm serious. Marriage isn't always about what you want, you have to compromise—"

"He traded me for a dog," Rosalind said, tossing giblets into a stockpot.

"I just hope you know what you're doing."

"I do," Rosalind told her with what she hoped sounded like certainty.

"Well, if you go down that road you have to take care of yourself. Cal's family is rich. He makes a good income."

"So?"

"So. How much do you make at that place? Can you support yourself?"

"I'm not going after alimony if that's what you mean," Rosalind insisted, lining giblets up on a cutting board.

"Don't get all Buddhist about it. Not now," Hermione advised.

"It's not like we have anything. Just a bunch of Ikea shelves and furniture from the Goodwill."

"You *never* bought real furniture?" Hermione asked, barely able to conceal her horror.

"We took vacations instead. And put money into the baby fund."

"What's happening to that?"

"Split it down the middle, I guess." The thought of it all made her weak. "I'm leaving all the furniture."

"Rosalind!"

"It's all crap. I'm streamlining, anyway."

"Streamline on E-Bay."

There was a crash from upstairs where Polly was loudly packing her belongings. She had briefly surveyed the kitchen that morning and refused to take anything out of a refrigerator involved in the "turkey holocaust." She was exacting punishment on her family by moving out, though her plan, as usual, wasn't entirely clear. A box clattered against the wooden floor above them. Hermione laughed and rolled her eyes.

"She doesn't mind when mom makes chicken," Rosalind said. "I think her wine bar even serves foie gras."

"I love foie gras! So does Laurent. We should go there before we leave."

"You can see the grapes I painted," Rosalind told her.

"That's right! Though it is pretty awful what they do," she said, staring down at the turkey guiltily. "To get foie gras."

"Yeah. Poultry in general," Rosalind agreed.

"I know! It's horrible. Should we brine it?"

"I think you have to brine the day before," Rosalind said. The sisters stared at the big, fleshy carcass in a roasting pan, like a child they'd just murdered, its dimpled pink legs taunting them.

"I read this article about turkey farms in Virginia. I think it was Virginia," Hermione said. "They're awful."

"Yeah, I know…"

"I think if we just cover it in butter," Hermione decided. "That's what Laurent's mom does. And the French are always right. At least when it comes to poultry. And butter."

"Goebbels. Mengele," Polly said, leaning against the door's frame. It wasn't clear how long she'd been standing there.

"Polly, don't be silly," Hermione said. "It's our last Thanksgiving in the house. Besides, you minimize the Holocaust saying crap like that."

Polly rolled her eyes. "I just came down for more boxes."

"Be sure to bring them back when you're done. Mom and Dad'll need them when they move," Rosalind said.

"They're never moving," Polly said emphatically.

"I think they really are," Hermione said, wiping her hands on a paper towel. "Has anyone ever met this woman?"

"I think I've seen her walk back to his studio. That's usually what he does with girlfriends," Polly told them.

"He's had girlfriends?" Hermione asked, incredulous.

"Duh," Polly sighed. "Do you guys really think mom and dad have been celibate for, what, twenty years? Seriously?"

"Well, yeah," said Hermione.

"Dad hasn't been. Don't know about mom," Polly admitted.

"D'you know, Ros? Didn't Polly say she was seeing someone in your tango class?" Hermione pressed.

"I think it was a flirtation. He's a Republican," Rosalind equivocated. "How far could it go?"

A hush fell across the room as the girls silently contemplated Helen and a Republican.

"Maybe he makes her happy," Hermione finally said.

"Puhleaz," Polly said. "They have one conversation about gay marriage and it's over."

"Maybe he supports it," Hermione offered. "Where's he on gay marriage?" she asked, turning to Rosalind.

Rosalind shrugged. "He's OK with the gay guys in class. Sorta."

"It's no big deal. I mean, Laurent's kinda conservative," Hermione said, returning to the turkey, spreading butter over its breast.

"What?" Polly asked.

"He's for gay marriage. That's not even an issue with him. It's more immigration and stuff. I mean, you should see Paris. It's overrun with immigrants."

"Um, I'm sorry but... aren't *you* an immigrant," Polly asked pointedly, she was electric with excitement, knowing precisely what her sister would say next.

"It's not the same," Hermione said.

"Because you're white?" Polly pounced.

"No! Because I'm educated. I have a job. I pay taxes. Don't put words in my mouth," Hermione said, gesticulating angrily with her butter-covered hands.

"You're a racist married to a fascist. Yeah. Europe — so totally progressive," Polly exclaimed.

"Oh, my God! All you do is point fingers and label people. The world is a lot more complicated than you realize — something you might find out if you ever moved out of mommy and daddy's house and had to fend for yourself."

"What do you think I'm doing?"

"I think you're making a big, crybaby stink, storming around and packing boxes which you'll never actually move until this house is sold out from under you. And then mom will take care of you. As usual!"

"She won't. I'm getting a place of my own," Polly told her.

"With what? You owe your entire salary to that seed company," Hermione reminded her.

"I'm moving in with Julian," Polly sneered.

"You are?" Rosalind asked, surprised.

"Yeah. Why wouldn't we?"

"I didn't know he wanted a roommate."

"We're not roommates," Polly said, exasperated. "We're *lovers*."

"Serious?!"

Polly gave her sister a long aggrieved stare. "Why wouldn't we be?"

"I thought he was gay," Rosalind said.

Polly raked a hand through her hair, exhausted by such a thoroughly tiresome family. "Because he knows wine? Jeez, Ros. Stereotype much?"

Even though Polly threatened a boycott she stayed for Thanksgiving, not because she wanted to, but because she could more soundly register her disapproval if she were actually there. What's more, she needed to save the family from the "big, dumb, oaky Chardonnays" they would inevitably drink with dinner if not for her intervention. The Plumley Thanksgiving usually consisted only of Rosalind, Cal, Polly, Helen, Richard and an eggplant casserole, but this one featured Eric, Laurent, Julian and a butter soaked turkey. Both Julian and Polly immediately dismissed the wine Eric dutifully brought as everything that was wrong with America.

"It's these big wines," Julian said indignantly. "They're these ripe, full-of-alcohol fruit bombs." He shook his head. Polly shook her head with him. "And they're affecting how other countries make their wines," he said, turning his attention to Laurent. "France, Italy, they're changing the way they make wines to cater to the American palate. It's really tragic."

Laurent smiled. He didn't know much about wine but he didn't like being lectured by an American about it. "If it's what the market wants…" he said, extending his arm, affecting a tone of profound reason.

"That's just the problem!" Polly complained. "The American palate pushes everything to this horrible, sweet, ripe end and these wines lose their complexity. It's grape juice! There's no balance, no structure to them — it sucks. What?" she asked, turning to a laughing Hermione.

"Nothing," Hermione said, controlling her laughter. "Weren't you, like, just vandalizing seed companies a few months ago?"

"I was taking action," Polly said. "You don't care. But what about your baby? Doesn't she matter? I mean, just think of all the hormones you're exposing her to just eating that turkey."

"It's organic," Helen told her.

"What does that mean? That means nothing," Polly shot back.

"Polly, please, let's not make this about the turkey again," Helen said.

"I can't believe all the lies people want to live with. It makes me crazy!" Polly said, inflamed with conviction. Julian poured her more wine and smiled at her. Rosalind could see he was enjoying this, in fact, found her extreme opinions — as was often the case with men and Polly — to be a bit of turn on. Polly and Julian as a couple had mystified her but on reflection it made sense. Polly had a tendency to become an extreme version of some aspect of herself for men. With Julian her look had changed, her nails were still black but were neat and manicured, her hair cut in a sleek black Louise Brooks bob. And she had — how could Rosalind have discounted it before? — recently mentioned that there were actually some quite decent wines from California. Polly insisted the wine bar had made her *more* socially conscious, talking loudly and often of her new best friends, Cesar and Fernando, the busboys. "I've learned so much about this town from them," she'd told Rosalind. "You wanna know a city, ask a busboy."

"You know that seed company you're so concerned about?" Polly asked Hermione. "They come up with a new strain of seed resistant to fungus, resistant to pests. Hmmm. It kills bees and caterpillars and bugs and fungus, so what does it do to humans? What would it do to a fetus? Nobody knows! They don't test it. They don't care. And when you buy a tomato in a supermarket you don't know if it's one of those or not. It's not even labeled. You could eat one in a restaurant and *never know*. Nobody's bothered by that? Really?"

Polly was particularly vexing when she made a good point. Hermione gave a conciliatory nod.

"Still," Laurent said, wading unwisely into the deep end of a Plumley debate, "there are other ways of making a change."

"Change from within is bullshit," Polly said.

"That's not true," Richard weighed in. He had been enjoying his turkey, quietly letting the noise of his family wash over him. "Gandhi, Mandela, King. You saying their change was bullshit?"

"No, but —"

"Name one good thing Leon Czolgosz accomplished," he demanded.

"Who?"

"You see?" Richard said turning to Laurent like his own personal tour guide. "Exactly the problem with America: we know our opinions but we don't know our history. Leon Czolgosz. The anarchist who assassinated President McKinley. Name one good thing that resulted from his violence."

"That's not a fair comparison," Polly huffed.

"Why?" he asked. "Because you don't know who he is or because you disagree with anarchy?"

"What about the bees?" Polly protested.

"I'm not talking about the bees," Richard countered.

"You don't care about them?"

"I care more about my daughter being able to follow a logical train of thought," he said, setting down his fork and lacing his fingers in front of him.

"Richard," Helen said, "Don't be patronizing."

"I'm not patronizing!" he protested.

"Well, now you're patronizing *me*," Helen said with an aggrieved sigh, the superior sigh of a master, the kind of sigh at which Polly was still a rank amateur.

"That's bullshit," he said, returning to his turkey.

"You're being a bully," Helen exclaimed. "And McKinley was succeeded by Roosevelt who started the national parks and the environmental movement."

Richard studied her, his face frozen in a look of decades-long irritation. "Not everything is a feminist moment," he told her.

"I didn't say it was."

"You implied."

"Well," Helen said acidly, "*As a man*, I guess you would know."

Richard and Helen stared across the table at one another. Only Polly continued to eat.

"I'm sorry I have a girlfriend. Is that what you want me to say?" Richard finally said.

"Do you think I care? After all this time?"

"Don't you?" he asked.

"I actually have a lover of my own," she said.

"The Republican?" Polly gasped.

"He did vote Romney, which I'm not happy about, but the sex is good and there it is."

Rosalind looked around the table, unsure whether the looks of surprise were for the sex or Romney.

"Think I'm going to have pie in my study," Helen resolved quietly, setting down her wineglass and rising, taking her plate into the kitchen. The silent table could hear her cut out a piece of pumpkin pie and then the sound of the door to her study shut. Their eyes all turned to Richard, who sat quietly finishing his dinner.

"The turkey's very good," he said to Rosalind and Hermione. "Very moist."

"Thanks," Rosalind managed to say.

"Yes. Very moist," Eric said, nodding. She could feel him next to her silently reconsidering their relationship.

"We used a lot of butter," Hermione added and everyone voiced their approval, pushing food around on their plates. Richard broke the awful silence.

"Think I'll take my pie in the studio," he said then repeating with nearly perfect accuracy Helen's sounds in the kitchen. There was the knife's slice and then an unmistakable high screech as the knife scraped the pie up and onto a dessert plate. The sound seemed to stretch and travel and enclose the listening daughters and their companions and, for Rosalind at least, marked the moment her family, as she knew it, came to an end.

He took his plate and a cup of black coffee out into the night, traversing the lawn in great long-legged strides. The light in the little studio came on.

"Nice job," Hermione told Polly.

"I didn't do anything," Polly said, uttering the phrase she'd used since the day she could speak.

"Just because of the turkey," Hermione said, shaking her head in disbelief, "you had to ruin everything."

The party broke up. Hermione was tired and Laurent followed her upstairs to bed. Polly and Julian had a party to go to. Eric and Rosalind drove home in silence. When they arrived at the house Rosalind fully expected Eric to bolt to the bedroom and start packing her clothes. They had brought home their ripe dumb wine and Eric opened it, setting a glass in front of her, clearly bracing her for the worst. Rosalind took a sip. Now that Polly had brought it to her attention it *did* taste too sweet and smelled too heavily of alcohol. Eric took a deep sip of the wine.

"Not bad," he pronounced, pleasantly surprised.

"Yeah," Rosalind agreed absently, drinking again, girding herself for the inevitable.

"I think — " Eric began and then took another drink, straightening his back and turning to her, " — we should get married."

"Really?"

"Why not?"

"I kind of figured after that three ring circus…"

"I want us to be married."

Rosalind stared at him, amazed. "I'm not even divorced yet."

"We'll have to change that."

Rosalind looked down at her hand cradled now in his.

"Don't you want to?" he asked.

Rosalind was almost ready to accept her divorce in the abstract, but when it came to trips to the county courthouse for forms and petitions, her nerves failed. She and Cal hadn't even officially talked about it. She could only assume that theirs would be a no-fault divorce with no disputes. The avoidance of the topic unbroken by any action was typical of their marriage; filing for divorce was like any other domestic chore they left undone until eventually one of them broke down and scrubbed the bathtub or threw out those molding things in the fridge.

"Of course," she explained. "Everything's just happening so *fast*."

"But that's what's so great!"

"Why do we even have to get married?" she wondered aloud.

"Because," he said simply, "we're in love. Aren't we?"

Rosalind nodded. "Of course we are. I just want to be intelligent about this," she said, searching his eyes for doubt. There wasn't any. Eric Ames was a man of certain and sudden convictions: he'd gone from dancer to math teacher in the space of a week and now he wanted to get married. His feeling was so strong it was almost enough for two people, Rosalind reasoned. But surely people didn't get married just because one person had the courage to ask, did they? She closed her hand as though wrapping his question inside it. He seemed disappointed by her reticence, annoyed even. He hated being impulsive alone. She kissed his hands, his long ink-stained fingers and thanked him. She would have to think about it.

twenty five

ROSALIND FINALLY SAW HER: the mysterious ceramicist. Helen was on campus teaching that day. Rosalind had stopped by the Plumley house to go through her mother's cookbook collection, thinking she'd make something special for Eric to appease and distract him while he waited for her answer. Marriage seemed a rash response to a divorce. But then, it seemed like everyone was doing it. She looked out the kitchen window and saw her father's girlfriend loping across the wet grass to his studio. She was tall and slim and wore dark jeans, a blue ski-vest and had long grey-black hair loosely collected in a barrette at the nape of her neck. She knocked at the studio door and without waiting for a response let herself in. Cozy, Rosalind thought as she tucked the *Silver Palate Cookbook* into her bag and wandered outside.

Curiosity and a sudden resolve that everyone in the family needed to grow the hell up emboldened her to knock at the studio door. A murmur of voices and then the door swung open.

"Rosalind!" her father said, registering his surprise.

"I was getting a cookbook," she said, gesturing to her bag for corroboration, "and saw your friend and thought I should meet her." She gave her father a long, penetrating stare to indicate she meant no harm, in fact wanted to establish what could at least ostensibly be mistaken for normalcy. He gave a slight glint of a smile and turned his body, allowing her inside. The woman rose and smiled warmly, offering her hand.

"You must be Rosalind. I'm so happy to meet you." She actually seemed to mean it. "I'm Katherine. I hope we can get to know each other."

Was it disloyal of Rosalind to suddenly wish the same thing? Should she feel guilty that this woman's manner put her so at ease that she was already wanting to suggest lunch so she could discuss her problems?

"Hi, Katherine. It's nice to meet you too. Finally." This last jab was for her father and he took it gamely. Rosalind took her in. Her father could search the world and all its peoples and nations and he would not find as near an opposite to Helen as this woman. She was calm, unflappable, still. She emanated a kind of serene grace that made Rosalind fully expect wild birds to land on her shoulder and whisper secrets in her ear. Rosalind noticed her father smiling; he seemed boyish and stupidly happy. Good for him, she thought.

"I hear you're a ceramicist," Rosalind said.

"And a very talented one," Richard told her.

Katherine smiled teasingly at him. "I'm very lucky to have work I love," she said. "And I hear you're a very talented painter."

"You've been told lies," Rosalind said, rolling her eyes in self-deprecation.

"What?!" Richard asked. His voice was so intense she'd thought he was joking until she turned to see his stricken expression. "Don't say that about yourself. Ever. You are very talented."

Rosalind leaned in conspiratorially to Katherine, "I paint flowers and birds," she explained.

"Didn't you paint those grapes?" Katherine asked, turning to Richard for confirmation.

"Yeah. Those grapes are extraordinary, Rosalind," Richard told her. "Really. Incredible."

"Really?" Rosalind asked. She could feel herself start to blush.

"Yeah," he said, "we were in last week visiting Polly, well, checking up on Polly." They all laughed. "I was knocked out. It's the first time you've made something beautiful without apologizing for it."

"*Really?*" Rosalind had to ask again. She couldn't believe it. They were sexy grapes. That's all.

"So beautiful," Katherine agreed, "Almost like stained glass."

"That's what I was going for," Rosalind said. Lunch! They had to have lunch.

"Really just beautiful," Richard told her conclusively.

"Well," Rosalind said, recovering, "thanks."

Rosalind noticed Katherine and her father exchange a significant look.

"I should be getting on my way," she told them both.

"I'm not staying," Rosalind assured her.

"No, no — I've got a store in North Portland selling my stuff I owe a visit. Wanna get over there before afternoon traffic. I'll let you two alone."

She left as quietly as she'd arrived. Rosalind and Richard sat in the studio, a light rain rattling across the roof.

"Well," he said. "That's Katherine."

"She seems really nice."

"She is," he said, nodding emphatically.

More silence. Rosalind moved to leave, sensing her father wanted to be alone.

"I didn't do this without thinking," he said.

"Sorry?"

"I wouldn't just leave your mother."

"Dad. It's fine. Really."

"I just," he searched the room, studying his own painting, "I want you to know you all are very important and I do nothing lightly. Nothing."

"I know. I know that."

"It's just," he stared forward still, "the cancer's back."

"Oh." Rosalind moved back from the door and sat down. Her father wouldn't look at her, was busy working through what he needed to say.

"It's back and we don't know how bad yet, but there may be surgery which could leave me incontinent or impotent or much better or not changed at all." He exhaled slowly.

"I'm sorry."

"Yeah, well, so... I knew things couldn't stay the same. I couldn't live like we were. I'm in love," he said and fixed his daughter with a look of wonder.

"I understand."

"I know you do. You're the only one that would." He turned to her, shaking his head, addled by the strangeness that life kept throwing at him. "Are you in love?"

"I don't know," Rosalind admitted. "I mean, yes, but he's asked me to marry him."

Richard laughed. He patted her shoulder awkwardly.

"What?" she asked.

"*One is in greatest danger*," he said, "*of being run over when one has just got out of the way of a carriage.* Nietzsche."

Rosalind laughed. "You should talk." They both laughed now and as their laughter faded Rosalind grew serious. "Get the surgery. If you have to. Whatever it takes. Please?"

He turned to her and smiled. "OK. And you paint. Men come and go," he said wagging a finger. "Be good to yourself. What you have? Inside? That's permanent. Any man doesn't see that, doesn't deserve you."

"That's sweet."

"I mean it!"

Rosalind nodded, trying to produce a smile that would reassure him.

"Are you taking good care of yourself?" he asked. Was she?

"I am," she assured him. "I'm trying."

twenty six

THERE WAS A TIME WHEN the honeymoon game was relatively easy to play. Honeymooners once came in three varieties: Oregon Coast, Hawaii, and Disneyland. Oregon Coast honeymooners were either the arty, poor types or the kinds of people who hailed from the fringes of Portland, had teeth missing from a meth habit or held a vocational degree from one of the schools that advertised during *Perry Mason* reruns. Hawaii honeymooners were moneyed with parents that were usually either doctors or bankers. They were blandly attractive with new degrees from the University of Oregon — or even sometimes, Stanford — in business administration or communications. Disneyland honeymooners were Oregon Coast honeymooners who somehow happened into a few thousand dollars, either through an inheritance or an improbable scratch-off win, and were shooting the wad to see Mickey. They would probably soon have gambling and drug addictions and spend the rest of their lives arguing about child support.

Rosalind had played this game since she was a teenager, she'd invented it herself, spreading out the Sunday paper and guessing from a photo where a couple was headed. Helen had chided her that it was all based on classist assumptions, which was precisely the point. But now people went to Mexico or Europe or backpacked in Montana or China. They went to Vietnam and Turkey and Brazil. There were so many new types of honeymooners that had moved into the area over the decades. It made Sundays even more challenging.

Morning light streamed into the breakfast nook as Rosalind unpacked the ever-thinning Sunday paper, throwing out advertisements, nearly half the bulk, and went searching for the wedding announcements. Eric had left to run errands for the morning, leaving her alone with coffee and an empty house. She found the section, thinking what kind of honeymoon she and Eric would take. Maybe Buenos Aires. She hadn't agreed to the engagement yet. She didn't know why but for some reason she wasn't saying "yes."

She had driven downtown under sheets of rain, running to the courthouse and filing the necessary paperwork to set her divorce in motion. Her mother had offered to go with her. They could file together she'd suggested with a kind of mordant cheeriness. Rosalind declined. It was enough that she had to occasionally dance the tango with her mother — joint divorce was as good a place as any to draw the line. Afterwards, she went to the Heathman Hotel's bar and ordered a martini in the middle of the day. She had never done that before, but she imagined it was the slightly worldly, slightly sad thing a woman should do after filing for divorce. She drank half of it, the gin salty with olive juice burning her throat before realizing how sad it actually all was: the wet raincoat, the gin, the divorce. She ordered another and spent the next hour in the ladies room crying. She told Eric that she'd run into a college friend downtown and had a cocktail. She told him she'd filed for divorce and felt nothing but freedom and happiness and roads leading to sunshine. She told him she'd be free in ninety days.

She opened the newspaper. The first couple was easy. Permed hair and methamphetamine eyes. Oregon Coast. Maybe today wouldn't even be a challenge after all. The second couple was more difficult. She had just graduated from Oberlin with a degree in music. He had a history degree from Yale and was working on a doctorate. These were tricky. Europe probably. Maybe Latin America? Folks were getting more and more inventive. Rosalind gave up, scanning down to the bottom of the announcement for the answer. Belize. Belize? Who knew? She and Cal had settled for a few days camping on the Salmon River. They were young and broke and prided themselves on the simplicity of their honeymoon, though if Rosalind were being honest, Venice or Paris would have been more to her liking. But she was young and still trying to be the intrepid, unpretentious bride her new husband admired so much.

She looked across the page. There were a lot of December weddings going on. She noticed another couple, matching smiles, almost acrylic in their sharp good looks and intense happiness. They had the kind of happiness that looked like gloating. Rosalind immediately resented it. She guessed Hawaii. She was right. Some things never changed. She moved on to another couple but her eyes kept ticking back to Hawaii. She studied their faces and then read the announcement and then realized: the name, Janine Stauffer. Eric's ex-wife. She felt her heart race. She looked around her at the tastefully painted walls and the bamboo floors. Everything was Janine. Still. Everything always came back to Janine.

"Maybe we could go dancing tonight. What do you think?" Eric asked, coming through the kitchen door, his arms full of groceries. Rosalind looked up from the paper.

"You didn't tell me Janine got married," she managed to say.

"Oh, yeah." He didn't look at her, just kept putting away groceries.

"When did you find out?"

"I don't know…"

"No, really. When did you find out?"

"Why does it matter?" he asked, a little irritated.

"I just think it's weird you never mentioned it is all."

Eric turned and leaned against the counter, facing her. "A while ago."

He frowned. "Why?"

"I'm wondering if your proposing had anything to do with her getting married?" she said.

"How could it?"

"How could it not?"

"What are you saying?"

"I'm saying that you're not over her and you're in some weird competition where if she gets married you do too."

"That doesn't make sense."

"The timing's a little weird, don't you think?" she said.

"No," Eric said, still senselessly holding a carton of milk in his hands.

"So it's just purely coincidental?"

He looked at her squarely. "It's purely coincidental."

Rosalind watched him sadly as he put the milk away and took a seat next to her, cradling her hands in his.

"What's going on?" he asked gravely.

"You're not ready for this," she told him.

"Yes, I am."

"You're not and I'm not. Look at these people," she said, gesturing to the sheet of smiling couples staring up at them from the newspaper. "You won't even let me paint the walls!"

"You're making up reasons for us not to be together. Why?"

"I don't know," she said.

Eric exhaled deeply. He took her hands in his. She noticed the black ink marks on his fingers and felt a pang of nostalgia.

"Listen," he said, his voice measured and clear. "I've been hurt, you've been hurt. Everyone's been hurt. The question is what do you want to do about it? Do you want to go around being hurt forever?"

"No, but —"

"You can come up with all kinds of reasons to not love me or for me to not love you, but at some point you've got to dive into the deep end with me or stay where you are. What do you *want*?"

"I want my life back," Rosalind finally managed. "I want a life that I recognize as my own again."

"And this isn't it?" asked Eric.

"I don't know."

"You miss Cal. That's fine. I miss Janine sometimes. But it's not the end of the world. It's just grief. Won't kill you. You want me to paint *that* on the walls? I'll do it."

Rosalind nodded, appreciating the sentiment but realizing it was all much bigger than painting walls.

"I'm lost," she said, her voice welling with emotion. "I didn't know how much until just now. I guess I hoped I could distract myself enough and it would go away. It didn't."

"What're you saying?" he asked, wrapping his arms around himself defensively.

"I need to go home. I want to go home."

"To Cal?"

"No. *Home*."

"But you are home."

"That's the thing: you *don't* know me. And we haven't 'always been together.' It's like we're both hiding out from our lives together. That's not something you can do forever. Or at least I can't."

Eric nodded, not because he agreed, but he could see there was no point in disagreeing when someone had made up her mind — he'd learnt that much from his divorce.

After she packed her few bags into the back of her car and hugged him, Rosalind never saw him again. After a few weeks it was like she'd never known him at all, like summer friendships she'd strike up as a child when the family stayed a few weeks at the beach or another city. The friendship was site specific. She couldn't miss it any more than she'd miss the Eiffel Tower in her backyard. It was where it belonged, somewhere in the past.

twenty seven

Vinyl, eight track tapes, audiocassettes, and CDs. Cancelled checks from the eighties and the nineties, magazines dating back to the early seventies. Children's books and gender neutral toys; a child's ice skates; Rosalind's dollhouse and Barbie dolls (resisted by Helen). Matchbox cars and luggage; chess sets and backgammon. Newspaper and magazine clippings of every single article, sometimes with extra copies, that either Helen or Richard had found interesting. A Yuban Coffee can full of foreign coins, once magical to the Plumley girls, once hidden and fought over like buried treasure, now forgotten; wrapping paper and rubber bands and roller blades and typewriters and coloring books and uncapped pens dried out since the Reagan administration. Here were the tar pits of the Plumley family, its unearthed remains. The basement.

Richard had carved out an orderly room separated by temporary walls purchased from a hardware store decades ago. The rest was landfill. They joked it was the Hotel California: things checked in but could never leave. Nothing had ever been thrown away. Nothing. The tar pits were just something the Plumleys scooted past as they headed towards the washing machine. No order had ever been imposed until the day Rosalind and

Helen ventured down like miners, listening for sounds of implosion as they slowly burrowed a path deep into the detritus.

"I thought you or Hermione might want it. When you have your own kids," Helen would explain each time Rosalind accusingly held up another antiquity.

"Hermione and I aren't going to need your cancelled checks from the eighties, Mom," Rosalind sighed.

"We might need those for taxes."

"You only need to hang on to financial records for three years."

"I didn't know that," Helen said, genuinely surprised.

"How do you not know that?"

Helen raised her hands, exasperated. She'd had other things on her mind, that's how.

"I can't believe your father left all this for us to do," Helen said, surveying the mounds of crap as though it were something that had been done to her.

"You told him to."

"Well," Helen said, fingering a yellowed news article from the nineties about prostate cancer, "he didn't have to *accept*."

Rosalind rolled her eyes, trying to get the operation back on track. "Surgical, Mom. Surgical strike, that's what we're doing: Go in, throw away, get out."

"Are you ever going to tell me what happened with Eric?"

"I told you. It didn't work out," Rosalind said.

Helen shook her head skeptically.

"I don't know what the hurry is going through all this. This house isn't going to sell anytime soon."

"Not with a basement full of junk," Rosalind said, trying to rally her.

"Do you remember these ice skates?" Helen asked holding up what appeared to be the smallest ice skates in the world.

"Surgical strike, Mom. No nostalgia," Rosalind reminded her.

"I said you were too young but Richard said it was fine. He was right," she recalled wistfully. Richard had moved into Katherine's house just before Christmas. Helen had pretended not to care, but Rosalind had detected more nostalgic detours like this than usual.

"You know, it's not that I resent his finding someone new. I really don't, after all this time. I just didn't think he'd want a divorce the *minute* he qualified for Medicare. You know? It's a little... unromantic. Even for him."

"Well," Rosalind said gently, resolving to tackle the basement on her own later. "Maybe there are other reasons."

"Is that what he told you?"

"It's just, people have their reasons. You never know," Rosalind said, taking in the basement. Their efforts amounted to only one small pile for the Goodwill. "He went through a lot with the cancer—"

"We all did!"

"I know, but maybe he's just realizing he isn't here forever. That changes people."

Helen nodded, conceding she may have a point and anyway, what was the use in worrying about it now?

"I wonder if Hermione would want these ice skates," Helen speculated, holding them up to the light. Rosalind felt a twinge of resentment; Helen hadn't been the least bit interested when she was pregnant.

"What about me?" Rosalind asked.

"Oh, you don't want to go messing up your life with babies. They're awful."

"Thanks."

"You have to wait years before they say anything interesting. People sentimentalize motherhood but it's really more like joining the army."

Rosalind nodded. She could feel emotion surging in her chest and the slow creep of feeling gutted by loss and grief.

"Let's get rid of stuff!" Rosalind said, trying to shore up her resolve.

For someone who professed to see motherhood unsentimentally, Helen turned out to be far more sentimental than Rosalind would have guessed, insisting on saving every report card, every crafts project the girls had brought home over the decades. Rosalind would sneak what she could into the recycling bins, regarding Monday, recycling day, with a kind of holy ardor. Each Monday the weight lessened, the pieces of the past carried away by the tide of those lovely, loud trucks.

Evenings were often spent over long meals and bottles of red wine with Helen and her friend, Karin.

"We're playing opposite world," Helen informed Rosalind one night.

"In opposite world older women are highly sought after by hot young things —" Karin explained.

"Have you seen this woman Rushdie was married to? She's absolutely stunning," Helen said. She had just been given Padma Lakshmi's cookbook and couldn't get over it. "These guys!" she hooted. "They look like gnarled old trees for chrissakes. Rupert Murdoch. Norman Mailer, well, he's dead now, but still... Can you *imagine* a world where a woman is average looking —"

"Or fat!" Karin added.

"— Or old but keeps getting beautiful young things because she's brilliant or funny or powerful? Not that I aspire to be a man," Helen added. "But it's fun to play. What if Margaret Atwood and Hugh Jackman were an item? Who else? Gloria Steinem! Steinem and who? Who should we give her?" asked Helen. Karin poured herself more wine.

"Gerard Butler?" Karin suggested.

"Who's he?" Helen asked.

"I think he's the new James Bond," Karin answered.

"Rosalind," Helen said, waving with exasperation, "who's the new James Bond?"

"Daniel Craig."

Helen and Karin looked at each other quizzically.

"Then who's Gerard Butler?" Karin asked.

"Another actor," Rosalind said. She thought she should go upstairs; she didn't have the energy for them tonight.

"Who the fuck are these people? Paul Newman. Now, there's a movie star!" Karin exclaimed.

"I always liked Sean Connery," Helen said. "Nadine Gordimer. Who should we give her?" Helen asked.

"Brad Pitt?" Rosalind suggested. "They both care about Africa."

"A perfect match!" Helen crowed, patting Rosalind on the back.

Helen shrugged, pleased. "OK. Hillary Clinton. Let's give her someone young. Inappropriately young. Someone so young we probably don't know who he is. Help us out, Rosalind. Who's Liam Hemsworth? Why do I even know that name?"

"I don't know those actors either."

Karin thought about this, staring out the window at the black night. A steady rain had started to fall. "None of us knows who young actors are," she said.

"So?" Helen asked.

Karin cocked an eyebrow as though she'd made her own point. "The culture's passing us by. We're irrelevant."

"Fuck you," Helen said, pouring them all more wine. "I'm *extreeemely* relevant."

"You," Karin said, fixing Helen in her sights, "have a lover. I have nobody. I'm fifty nine and I have no one."

"Oh, well, hell," Helen exclaimed, "Sex is nice but it's not everything."

"Says the lady with a lover," Karin reminded.

"Paul?" Helen rolled her eyes, amused. "How long's that going to last?"

"Why?"

"He's in love with his dead wife. Besides, I'm still in the middle of a divorce. I don't wanna be tied down again. Let's get back to the game. Angela Merkel. What about her? Rosalind?"

Rosalind smiled but her heart wasn't in it. She was trying to be light and funny and jaded about life like Helen and Karin, but it wasn't working. Her thoughts kept drifting back to Cal and the miscarriage and the life they almost had. It haunted her. She excused herself and went upstairs to her bedroom. She flopped down on her bed, exhausted, and looked up at her mobile, gently swaying from a draft in the room, throwing shadows. Rain pelted the roof in a soothing, constant thrum. Here I am again, she told herself. Home again. She could still hear Helen and Karin arguing and laughing in the distance. She shut her eyes and tried to forget everything, all the things that shadowed her all day and into the night. She would be light; someday she would release all the clutter. She would be light.

twenty eight

HELEN PROVED TO BE MORE conventional than Rosalind would have expected. Paul never stayed the night, though he would come over often after tango classes with a group of old regulars like Kev and Andrew and Bethany and new members. Helen was always adding people. Rosalind had talked her into junking one of the couches in the room, a brown sectional from the eighties shredded down to its foundation by a succession of cats, which made way for a more generous dance floor. Helen had continued her studies of tango and Argentina, occasionally voicing an interest in visiting, especially now that she was taking classes from a real live Argentine who taught the intermediate class.

"Do you know we've been doing it all wrong?" Helen asked, exasperated and delighted at the same time. "We're not supposed to be learning steps at all! We've all been having to unlearn with Gustavo everything we learned with Barry and Mariela. Our first class we just walked around the room."

"Yeah, some men I danced with at the *milongas* said the same thing," Rosalind told her.

"Really? Why didn't you say anything?"

Rosalind only shrugged. Since moving out of Eric's place, Rosalind hadn't been back to a class or a *practica* and hadn't wanted to. Tango reminded her of him.

"Well, that's just silly," Helen told her, "it's not like the dance belongs to him."

Rosalind knew she was right, knew there was something even deeper that prevented her from going back. Since she began something had always bothered her about tango: she still had no idea how people knew what the hell they were doing. The dance had no agreed upon formula, no designated rules, just collectively shared sequences that a leader could use interchangeably. It was a conversation, not a speech. This was what was allegedly so wonderful about it: it was an improvisation, a negotiation between two people. No choreography, no predetermined pattern, just endless, unpredictable new formations. One couldn't dominate the other. It was — if not historically, at least ideally — a dance of equals. This struck her as lovely in principle and crazy-making in practice. How do you know what to do? "The man will lead you," her teachers told her. What if his lead doesn't make sense? "It will. Practice!" Mariela had instructed brightly, unhelpfully.

Rosalind had managed to fake it the first few months, moving fleet and confident for a few seconds before crashing to earth, stumbling over a partner's foot, stopping when he wanted her to move, moving when he didn't. She had hoped at some point it would all click. It was like learning a language, she told herself. You learn words and phrases, verbs and tenses and you repeat them nonsensically, full in the faith that one day, wonder of wonders, you'll be having a conversation. But tango never clicked. Never clicked, that is, with anyone but Eric.

Helen would push Rosalind to dance on the nights the class came back to the house, and sometimes she'd relent, dancing unhappily with Kev or more easily with Andrew. They were all moving past her, getting better.

"Where'd you go?" a man asked her at one of these parties. Rosalind turned around to see Bobby of the tight dreadlocks and infectious smile she'd met in the beginning class.

"Oh! Hi," she said, startled.

"Haven't seen you in class," he said, leading her easily across the floor. "You're exactly the right height," he noticed approvingly.

"Thanks," she laughed. "I do what I can."

"How've you been?"

"OK."

"You don't sound too sure," he told her with a smile.

"Life's a little challenging sometimes."

Bobby laughed. "I hear ya."

"Is your girlfriend here?" she asked, eager to move off the topic of her life.

"We split up."

"Sorry to hear that," she told him as Kev and Andrew crashed into them.

"Sorry, man," Andrew said. Kev sailed on without stopping.

"Yeah, she went back to her ex," Bobby said leading Rosalind into a step she didn't know.

"I'm sorry, I don't know what I'm supposed to do," she said, looking down at their tangled feet.

"You're supposed to say: How's that possible, Bobby? How could anyone leave someone as great as you?"

Rosalind laughed self-consciously. "I meant the step."

"I know," he said smiling that smile. "I'm only fooling. Here," he said moving her deftly, slowly to his side as they did a step around one another. "You go like this and then this," he said, leading her through the new step.

"That's cool!" Rosalind told him.

"Yeah, right?" he enthused, leading into a basic step.

"And I don't know how someone could leave someone as great as you," she remembered to tell him.

"I know, right? What are we gonna do with these people, Rosalind?"

"You asked me that the first time we danced."

"I did?"

"You did," she admitted. The song ended and Bobby looked squarely at her.

"You want to dance the next one too?"

"Sure," she agreed.

She could dance indifferently, if competently, with Kev and Andrew and all the other men from her class. With Bobby she danced with intention. It felt like it was leading somewhere.

"I hear you used to go to the *practicas*," he said.

"Yeah. While ago."

"They scare me. Maybe we could go sometime?" he suggested.

"They seem scarier than they actually are. Sure," she made herself say, "how about next week?"

Bobby smiled his smile. "You're on, Rosalind."

"Do you ever see Cal?" Helen asked with studied casualness while they finished a cassoulet Helen had made one night.

"He traded me for a dog," Rosalind said, trying to shut the conversation down. Helen had a way of remembering all her own slights and forgetting everyone else's.

"Well... to be fair, he thinks the dog is his brother," she reasoned.

"But Jordy's dead!" Rosalind said, the emotion of it surprising her, "*I'm* alive."

"I know, but —"

"I don't want to talk about it."

Helen nodded patiently and poured herself more wine. "Any more?" she offered Rosalind.

"No, I'm good."

Helen nodded and they ate in silence.

"I was going to ask Hermione if she wants that dollhouse," Helen said finally.

"Oh, my God, seriously!" Rosalind erupted. It was *her* dollhouse, hard-won after a lengthy debate on gender roles with her mother.

"What?" Helen asked.

"How is it you're so supportive of Hermione and her pregnancy? Where was this when I was pregnant?"

"I was very supportive," Helen protested.

"No, you weren't. Not like with Hermione."

Helen inhaled sharply, weighing her words.

"Because she's *happy*. She and Laurent are happy. I didn't want you having a baby just because Cal's depressed."

"Cal became depressed after the miscarriage, not before."

"Oh," Helen said.

"Yeah. Oh." Rosalind said, clearing her plate. "Well, now I'm single and not pregnant. Happy?" Rosalind tossed dishes loudly in the sink. Helen joined her in the kitchen.

"Ros, I was only—"

"I don't want to hear how good your intentions were. You have no idea what I've been through — how awful it was to carry something inside you for weeks and weeks, to feel this weird intimacy and then to one day, suddenly have it all be gone." She started to weep.

"I'm sorry, darling. I'm so sorry. I didn't know." Helen put her arms around her.

Rosalind nodded and wept. "You don't know because you don't ask. Or if you do you never listen."

"OK, darling. I know." Helen held her as large, embarrassing sobs passed through Rosalind. She could smell the warm, animal smell of her mother. When was the last time she'd been held by her mother? Seven, eight years old. Certainly by nine Helen's embrace was mortifying to Rosalind. She didn't know what to feel, she was both uncomfortable and soothed.

"You just don't know what it's like."

"I'm listening," Helen said. "Tell me what it's like."

"It's like being on the phone with someone. You don't ever talk but you're communicating. Sometimes you hear breathing but mostly you just feel a presence, just there, all the time at the other end of the line. Then one day the line goes dead. There's no goodbye, no explanation, nothing that makes any sense. It's just you now, all day, walking through your day, hoping that that something at the other end will come back. And so you spend every day listening, really listening, to this dead line and going to bed every night feeling lost. And every day I have to get up and see these yoga mommies with their smoothies and their rich husbands and their meditation classes and I just think: if I'd only been calmer or did more breathing exercises or something I wouldn't have lost it."

"I had three pregnancies in the midst of total chaos, darling. If peace and lack of stress were a prerequisite for a successful pregnancy the planet would be empty."

"I know, it's just everyone is ready to tell you what you're doing wrong!" Rosalind protested, the tears welling back up. "I went to this fertility masseuse who told me I should've been wearing orange to open up my second chakra. Seriously. I mean, when you can't carry a baby *everyone* lines up to tell you what's wrong with you."

"They're idiots is all," Helen said, still stroking Rosalind's hand. Rosalind shook her head fiercely, worrying a thought out of it.

"The thing of it is, I never told you but when I was in New York I got pregnant," Rosalind said.

Helen nodded sympathetically. Tales of unplanned pregnancy were her forte.

"I didn't keep it, obviously. But it kind of messed me up. Emotionally. And now, I think sometimes that the reason I can't get or stay pregnant now is punishment for that."

"Oh, my dear, that's not true," Helen said, stroking Rosalind's hand.

"But what if it is? One of my tubes was blocked and they don't know why but think it's like this scar tissue from an infection of some kind. Either from the surgery or from something else, an infection I didn't know about, they don't know…"

"It's still not a punishment."

Tears streamed down Rosalind's cheeks again. "It feels like it is. I think sometimes that's why I keep working in a children's store even though I hate it and it just reminds me of everything that hurts inside. It's like

I'm a dog that shit the rug and now I'm just going to rub my nose in it to punish myself forever."

"Oh, darling," was all Helen could say for a long while.

"It's the first thing I think about when I wake up and the last thing I think of at night — that I was responsible for this really, really important thing and I fucked it up. I completely fucked up."

Helen took a deep, sad breath, patting Rosalind's hand resolutely and then walked to the kitchen, pulling a bottle from a back shelf and set it on the dining room table. She poured two glasses out.

"What I have to tell you requires excellent port," Helen told her dramatically.

"OK," Rosalind said warily.

Helen sat down, composed herself and stared at her glass of excellent port.

"When I found out I was pregnant with Polly, Richard and I were talking divorce — on the rare occasions we spoke at all — and I thought about not keeping her. So I know what you went through."

Rosalind nodded, a little stunned.

Helen sighed deeply. "She wasn't born into the kind of happiness you and Hermione were. I sometimes think it's why she's so angry all the time, so hard. I always felt bad about it for Polly. I guess that's why I indulged her a bit."

"Wow."

"The reason I'm telling you is this: No matter what your situation is, it's a hard choice. You never know what will come of it and you can't blame yourself. I felt in my bones that I should keep Polly but I know now part of that was hoping Richard and I would recapture some of what we had when you and Hermione were born. It didn't happen. I love Polly, I don't regret having her, but sometimes I do worry that her unhappiness is the result of all the turmoil around her when she was born. All the expectations we put on her. Unfairly. You just never know if you're doing the right thing. Never, ever. You just pick up and go on the best you can. I worried sometimes that you were doing the same thing with Cal, staying in it because you thought you should, not because you wanted to."

Rosalind pulled back from the table. "No. Cal and I were happy. We loved each other. I don't know what happened. I'm just no good at marriage."

"I don't want to hear any more of that shit. You worked hard at that marriage. You loved him and he loved you but it didn't work out. It's shitty but that's life. Everyone messes up at it. And if you want a baby that's great. We'll go out and get you some sperm tomorrow if you want."

Rosalind laughed.

"I'm serious," Helen continued. "Although we should get you someone young. I read in the *Times* paternal age increases risk of autism. We'll find you someone young, someone inappropriately young. You could have one on your own and move in here! We don't have to sell —"

"Mom," Rosalind said. "I'm not moving in here. And I'm not raising a kid with you."

Helen shrugged. Suit yourself. "In any case, you're not going back to that job. No daughter of mine's getting her face rubbed in anything, especially shit."

Rosalind smiled wearily. "What am I going to live on?"

Helen turned her palms to the air. "We'll find something."

"Ingrid's having her baby in a couple of weeks. I can't just quit."

"Lordy," Helen muttered, "all these women and their babies."

"Tell me about it."

"Listen. The world doesn't need any more babies. What it needs are women who don't spend all their time beating themselves up over shit they don't control. You're getting out of there. I'll talk to Richard, maybe he can get you in teaching at the art institute or something. We'll work it out," she said with a kind of convincing finality. "OK? I've let you down in the past. I know that," Helen's voice caught and Rosalind realized it was maybe the first moment she'd ever seen her mother subject to a truly unguarded emotion. Helen's eyes welled with tears. "I'm sorry."

"It's OK," Rosalind told her.

Helen took a deep breath and traced her finger along the Tibetan silk runner she kept on the dining room table.

"Richard and I always called you the *punisher*. We never had to discipline you. Not like we did Hermione or Polly. Because you were so hard on yourself. If there's anything I want for you now, as a mother, even if I don't 'deserve' it is: I want you to be gentle. I want you to have compassion. For yourself and everyone. It's what every parent wants. If they're any good. Which maybe I wasn't…"

Rosalind hugged her mother fiercely.

"You were good enough, mom. I knew you loved me. Even when you were weird."

"Which was often?"

"Which was often."

twenty nine

"THE BASTARD WANTS TWICE as much rent!" Ingrid announced. *little fig's* lease was up in less than sixty days. If Ingrid couldn't find a new store that fit her budget, she was just going to sell the inventory online and, as it turned out, that would be the end of Rosalind's employment. Apparently she wouldn't get the satisfaction of quitting after all.

"Don't bother painting any more of those," Ingrid told her when she'd sold the last hummingbird painting. "I mean, unless you want to. But I don't know if we'll be around next month."

Rosalind figured she might as well sell as many as she could before the store closed. Who knew when she'd see another paycheck? When she opened her father's studio she was surprised to see he'd left behind a bunch of his paints, including the one she'd borrowed for the sexy grapes. She should call him and ask if she could use them. She owed him a call; she still hadn't seen his new place or had that lunch with Katherine. She searched further and found he'd left behind, not too unsubtly, a stack of blank canvases, leaning provocatively against the wall. They were the wrong size for her hummingbird paintings, which she always did on a square. He hadn't left these behind by accident. It was no oversight; it was an invitation.

She took a long, assessing breath and stared at the stack of canvases. She could do hummingbird paintings in her sleep and sometimes, it seemed, even did. She painted in the background, noticing immediately she didn't really have the right colors for what she usually did. She'd just make do. She stood over the paints doing a quick inventory of what was available. One color caught her eye, a deep cornflower blue. It reminded her of the last bouquet of bachelor buttons and irises she'd bought Cal when it all fell apart. The saddest flowers in the world. She started to paint. When she thought to check the time two hours had past, her back hurt and she'd gotten two messages: one from Cal and one from Ingrid. She returned Ingrid's.

"Brilliant news!" Ingrid told her. "I found a place. It's cheap, it's cool, a little of a fixer upper but brilliant. And you are going to love the commute," she offered teasingly.

"Really? Where is it?"

"On the corner of your block."

She actually meant on the corner of Cal's block. Rosalind still hadn't told her about the split.

"That's great," Rosalind agreed unenthusiastically.

"Derek and I are buying the space. It's cheap. The owner had a heart attack and died and his daughter wants to unload it."

It was only then that Rosalind made the connection. "Is it a flower store?"

"Yes! It's a pit but it's got good bones. I was hoping you could do something creative with the walls."

"Sure, sure," Rosalind agreed. Poor Mr. Hoffman and his horrible daughter.

"Anyway! We'll talk more but I'm just so chuffed right now!" Ingrid said. "You're going to love it."

Rosalind painted one of the walls of the store turquoise with a branch with pale pink cherry blossoms stretching across it. Ingrid was rarely around since her doctor put her on bed rest after her blood pressure spiked.

"It's all the bloody stress," she explained wearily, taking in the developing store with pride.

She had offered to let Rosalind use the walls to display her paintings. The first painting, "The Saddest Flowers In The World," getting a prime spot behind the cash register, a tribute to the store's former life. She also kept up the sixties era *Flowers* sign on top of the building with the store's new name, *east fig,* painted brightly underneath. She had been surprisingly calm when Rosalind gave notice, assured by her willingness to wait until after the baby was born.

Cal stopped in after their first week. Rosalind was worried he would. She wasn't ready to see him. She wasn't sure how she felt about him anymore.

"Hey," he said nervously, trying to affect a casual air. "Place looks great!"

"Thanks. Yeah. Hello."

He looked at her painting over the register of the Saddest Flowers.

"He died, you know? Mr. Hoffman," she said, following his gaze.

"Really? Sorry to hear that."

"This is sort of my tribute to him," she said gesturing to the Saddest Flowers.

"It's really beautiful," he said, nodding. He looked good, Rosalind noticed. Healthier. He'd lost weight and seemed somehow unburdened.

"Thanks."

They both smiled wistfully.

"How's the dog?" Rosalind asked finally, searching for something, anything to talk about.

"He's fine. Ended up not doing the surgery after all. It's kind of controversial I found out. Tobin knows this great guy who does acupuncture on animals. Seems to be helping, so we'll see…"

"That's great."

"I know he's a dog, by the way. I do recognize that," Cal assured her. It seemed important to him that she hear it.

"Good," Rosalind said, nodding uncomfortably. "I'm glad."

"About the savings — you should have it. You can go to Argentina." It was the kind of magnanimous offer that seemed to want something in return. She wasn't sure what.

"That's not necessary. We'll split it," she said.

He shook his head dismissively. "But we should talk about the house. At some point. We need to decide what we want to do about it."

"Yeah."

"Are you free Thursday night?"

"Um, I guess. Yeah." She felt cornered. She was thinking more along the lines of coffee, during the day. "Oh, wait, no!" she said, remembering Thursday was the night she and Bobby were supposed to go to their first *practica* together.

"Oh," he said, not trying very hard to hide his disappointment.

"Another night?"

"It's just they're showing this movie and it's only playing Thursday. You should really see it. *The River*. Jean Renoir? There was a thing about it in the paper this morning, did you see that?"

She shook her head.

"Oh. Well, Scorsese says it's the most beautiful color film ever made. Along with *The Red Shoes*. So you should probably see it," he explained, as though the evening was more of an educational venture adding, in case she'd missed the point, "Cause, you know, you're into color."

"I'm really sorry. I have plans," she told him.

He nodded. "OK. No big deal. I just thought..." He stuffed his hands in his pockets, his eyes drifting toward the saddest flowers.

"You know —" Rosalind decided. "That's fine."

"What?"

"I'll shift my plans around."

"Really? Great. OK, then. I'll pick you up?"

"Let's just meet there."

She probably wouldn't have agreed to the movie had she known where it was screening: Cinema 21, an old revival house in NW Portland, the site of their first date. The choice was hardly an innocent act. She found him waiting in front of the theatre, his shoulders hunched, his breath forming clouds that floated up towards the marquee.

"I already got our tickets," he told her.

"Thanks," she said, following him up the stairs to the balcony, their usual spot.

The screening was sparsely attended, word about the film's status as the most beautiful color film had apparently not gotten out.

"It's supposed to be a new print!" he said. He got excited about these things. A movie was an awkward way to reconnect after so much time and drama but he was so eager to make it work that Rosalind tried to go along with it.

"That's great," she said. "You've seen it before?"

He shook his head. "I don't even really know what it's about."

The lights went down and the movie began. It was set in India and Scorsese hadn't lied, the fifties-era Technicolor gleamed in stunning, larger than life, eye-popping hues. The film centered on a British expat family living along the banks of a great blue glittering river. Two redheaded girls flitted across the screen in brilliant dresses of green and blue and orange. They had both fallen in love with a visitor, another redhead, crippled in the war. But it was the subplot with a younger brother that set both Cal and Rosalind on edge. The boy was entranced by snakes — dangerous, venomous snakes. In an early scene he befriends an ancient snake charmer in a marketplace. Rosalind could hear a worried moan escape from Cal, the kind of sound he made when he'd misplaced his keys.

They could both see where this was going and the knowledge of it filled the small space between them — a dark, sickening dread. Rosalind could feel Cal tighten and clench when the brother appeared, searching for a snake. The girls fought over the man. The younger sister, distracted, passes by the brother, searching for what she believes is true love. Cal let out a sigh. Rosalind thought to ask him if he'd like to go but it was too late. The sister returned to find her brother dead under a tree. Rosalind could feel Cal shaking in small rigid movements. Onscreen the family learned the terrible news. There was a funeral with white sheets and a blue rolling river. Cal buried his head in his hands. Rosalind turned to him just as he let out a great racketing sob. The awful sound filled the theatre followed by a wailing, "Oh!"

"Cal," Rosalind said, her hand on his back, "let's go."

"No."

"Cal —"

"I'm fine," he said.

"You're not."

"Let me stay," he asked.

Rosalind nodded reluctantly. The movie continued. The mother broke down in grief. The father comforted her. The girls both lost love. The mother had a baby. Another girl. The girls hear the news, they've just received letters from the man they thought they loved but now he's gone and they're wistful and happy and sad. They turn to the Ganges and watch it roll on.

Rosalind and Cal sat in their seats after the lights came up and the audience wandered back up the aisle, out of the theatre and into the night. They sat silently both wiping away tears, strangely soothed.

"That doesn't happen very often anymore," he told her when they'd settled into the bar of an Italian restaurant near the theatre. The bar was noisy, noisier than either of them would've liked for the conversation, but the effort of finding another place was too daunting. It had been decorated in anticipation of Valentine's Day with hearts and red cupids taped to the mirror above the bar.

"I've been seeing this therapist," he continued. "Tobin recommended him. He's doing this research on Complicated Grief Syndrome. That's what he says I have. He had me tape record what happened, describing everything I remember from that day. It's hard but I have to listen to it. He says I have to teach myself to grieve for Jordy and then put the grief away."

"Yeah?"

"Yeah. It's helped. I'm better. Not all better. But better. I can get through the day."

"That's great," she told him. He did seem better. His eyes looked alive. "I'm really happy to hear that."

"What about you?" he asked pointedly.

Rosalind took a deep breath and nodded. "It's been hard."

"Yeah," he said, exhaling softly. He reached for her hand and held it as they sat in silence, loud music pulsing around them, sitting side by side at the bar. Finally she gestured to her cell phone she'd left sitting on the bar.

"I'd put it away," she explained, "but Hermione was due yesterday."

"No kidding!" he exclaimed. "That's great — really great…"

Cal looked at himself in the mirror behind the bar, preparing what he had to say.

"I'm really sorry. What I put you through. I have no excuse. I'm sorry. It's like —" He stared at the mirror over the bar, trying to understand something himself, "It's like I was trying to make us so small that if I lost you, it wouldn't hurt. If that makes any sense. Anyway. I'm not smoking anymore."

"Good for you."

"Cigarettes or weed. Haven't seen Glen in ages."

"Really?" she asked, surprised.

"So," he continued, finishing what he'd prepared, "I'm happy for you. You look like you're doing great. And if Eric makes you happy, I'm happy too." That seemed to take something out of him; he was working hard at being generous.

Rosalind stared down at her drink.

"We're not together."

"Oh?" he asked brightly.

"I'm staying with my mom."

"OK! How's she doing?"

"Fine. She's selling the house. It sold faster than she thought it would so she's moving soon. Some millionaire who just moved here with his family," she said.

"Wow. No more unniversary parties," Cal mused fondly.

"Nope. She's doing a sabbatical in Buenos Aires."

"That's cool. You could finally go too."

Rosalind nodded, straightening up, "I might visit but I'm actually starting a new job soon. I'm teaching at the art institute. Picking up a couple painting classes with my dad. He's going in for surgery next week, actually. Prostate, again."

"Oh, Plum, I'm so sorry."

"I know. It sucks," she sighed. "We're gonna co-teach and I'll be there when he can't be," she said with a wistful shrug.

Cal reached for her hand and gave it a gentle squeeze.

"And if it all goes well, he's taking some of the money from the house sale and travelling down to Mexico for a while with Katherine. He's happy, actually. Happier than I've ever seen him."

"I'm glad to hear that."

She looked at him squarely. "Argentina wasn't just about me. It was about us being happy again. Getting us out of our ruts and...whatever..." she said, smiling wistfully.

Cal nodded as a heavy silence fell between them.

"I'm happy for you," he said finally. "You deserve to be happy."

"Thank you."

They both took large sips of their drinks aware that the conversation was taking on larger dimension. There was always something tender and battered about her and Cal. She couldn't tell if this was an ending or a beginning.

"I didn't tell you," she said, "my mom has a *boy-friend*. And he voted for Romney."

Cal choked on his drink.

"You're joking?"

"Nope. He's a nice guy but, yeah, Romney."

They laughed for a long time and then ordered another round.

"How'd she meet a Republican?"

"Tango."

He nodded.

"Maybe when you get back you could give me another dance lesson," he offered, emboldened.

"Oh, really?" she asked, smiling broadly, amused and nervous. "Maybe."

"I'm ready to try something new," he said.

Rosalind smiled. "I'm not quite sure how to answer that."

"You don't need to answer now," he said. He looked at her a long time.

"What?" she asked.

"Nothing. It's just really nice to see you."

Rosalind laughed softly and traced the edge of her glass with her finger.

"You too."

They finished their drinks, restless and shy with one another. He walked her back to her car. A fine mist of rain trickled steadily, nothing worth finding an umbrella for but enough to quicken their steps.

"Can I kiss you?" he asked as they reached her car.

She nodded and they stood in the awkward space between the car and the curb, leaning against the car door, kissing tentatively like new lovers.

She smiled shyly. "Weren't we supposed to talk about the house?"

Cal laughed and shook his head. "I just wanted an excuse to see you."

"I kinda had that idea," she nodded.

"Do you want to talk about the house?"

She shook her head.

"This was nice," he said, helping her into her car, although it was unclear if he was talking about the night or the kiss or the years that had led up to them.

"It was," she agreed, feeling a strange lightness.

"We can always try again," he said.

"Try what?"

"Us. A kid."

Rosalind hesitated.

"Think on it."

"OK."

She looked across the street and noticed a tree illuminated from below, its bare branches looking almost white against the black night. The harsh light seemed to be calling to her, announcing that something was happening.

"I'll be in touch," she told him.

"Sounds good. Take care."

They shared a brief, marital kiss before she got in her car. She drove to the Plumley house, driving with the windows down, the cold night air streaming wet across her face. When she got there the lights were all out. She hadn't remembered ever coming home with the house so dark. A note from Helen told her that she was visiting Paul that night and wouldn't be back until morning.

Rosalind took the opportunity to visit every room, noting each refrigerator hum and furnace sigh, as though the house were slumbering and snoring, preparing for its next life. She went to her mother's room, still filled with tall stacks of books, and then Polly's and Hermione's reduced, almost unbearably, to bed frame and bare mattress. She went to her own room where she'd finally thrown out those horrible shadowboxes, where only the sparest hint of life still remained, her mobile shifting barely perceptibly from an unseen draft. She visited her father's now emptied room and the rest of the basement, its slowly dwindling stacks of papers and children's games the last diminishing evidence of the lives that had unfolded there.

She wandered outside, the night dark and still. The rain had stopped and the sounds of the neighborhood were encased in fog. She found the swing set. She stood in the space between the trees, their massive branches hanging over her. She once believed she could talk to them, that they could understand her and respond. She looked up at their branches, wondering if maybe it were true. It was the space where the Plumley girls discovered a confusing echo, you lost your bearings here, you had to scream and laugh until your sisters relented, revealing themselves from their hiding places among the trees. You felt uniquely, savagely alone until they did.

She used to believe the trees would tell her what to do in times of trouble and so she stayed waiting for an answer, any answer, with a child's faith, hearing only the sound of her own breath. She sat down on the grass staring up at the blank slate of dark sky, her breath forming clouds against it. She let the cold wet seep into her clothes. She would listen forever if need be.

She felt her phone vibrate telling her she had a text and the text told her she had a niece: Helene Plumley-Brun. A spring of joy spread through her. It was enough to know she still could feel such a thing. There would be so much to do — phone calls and Skype sessions from the hospital, not to mention house cleaning and storage lockers and packing. She noted how quickly her joy turned to lists and decided instead to take pleasure in the fact of this new girl and this moment of quiet under the trees.

She knew Helen would return home soon with her own list, full of things to do. In the meantime there was the peace of the house breathing its memories in and out, a lone light in the kitchen keeping vigil. She put her phone away and took in the dark air, a light rain picking up again. The wind gusted through the high branches as they brushed against the house, making their own strange music. It was cold and she knew she should go in but something compelled her to wait a moment longer, until she could hear — faintly at first, but unmistakable — the wild shouts and laughter of the Plumley girls echoing in the night.

Acknowledgements

MANY PEOPLE WERE OF TREMENDOUS help throughout the writing of this book. My first debt of gratitude goes to the tango teachers at 3rd Street Dance Studio and *A Puro Tango* in Los Angeles. Their classes and the other students I met provided the bulk of my practical research into the tango and the delightfully strange experience of learning to dance with a bunch of strangers.

For their valuable feedback on early drafts I have to thank Paul Francis, Michaela Lowthian-Bancud, Clea Montville-Wood, and Paul Mandelbaum. Much gratitude as well to Alison Halstead-Reid for the wonderful cover design and to Amie Ziner for additional design assistance. A special thanks to those who indulged me with multiple readings of the manuscript as it evolved over the years always providing advice, humor and many, many insights: my sister Lisa Vandever-Levy, my dear friend Scot Zeller; and my husband Mike Brosnan for his loving support, keen editorial eye, and vast knowledge of wine.

Finally, thank you to my parents William (Bill) and Ruth (Peter) Vandever for their love and lifelong support. Their example has shown me the ultimate challenge of romantic and familial love and, in the end, its enduring grace.

Made in the USA
Middletown, DE
17 November 2016